Take the Reins, COWGIRL

CAVANAGH COWGIRLS ROMANCE - 1

VALERIE COMER

GreenWords Media

This is my command
— be strong and courageous!
Do not be afraid or discouraged.
For the Lord your God
is with you wherever you go.
Joshua 1:9 NLT

Free book?

Love cowboys? Me, too! That's why I'd like to offer you an ebook copy of *The Cowboy's Forever Crush* free as an introduction to the world of my Montana Ranches Christian Romance series. This story world encompasses the Saddle Springs series, the Cavanagh Cowboys series, the Sweet River Ranch series, and now the Cavanagh Cowgirls!.

Come on in and be lassoed by love!

https://valeriecomer.com/subscribe-crush

CHAPTER
One

"I don't know."

Seriously? Emma Cavanagh pivoted and glared at her twin sister. "You've had weeks to make a decision." Months, really.

Alexia shrugged. "It's just… I can't decide."

"Lex. It is a *color palette*, not a matter of life or death."

The builder, Brent Callahan, smiled as he looked between the two of them. How could this man stay calm when his schedule was about to go poof? Maybe he didn't mind, because Dad was footing the bill. But Brent seemed too ethical to take advantage of that. "I can squeeze a little more time for you, Alexia, but it means your unit will be completed last. I need to order materials today or be held up on the entire project. Emma, I've recorded your choices, and Vivienne—" Brent consulted his phone "—emailed me with hers yesterday."

"Okay."

Emma couldn't believe her twin. Not for the first time

1

in their 24 years, she'd like to grab Lex by the shoulders and shake some sense into her ridiculous head.

Brent pocketed his phone. "I'll get the materials on order that I can and, since we don't have decent internet up here yet, that means a trip into town. I'll be back shortly. Alexia, you have my email address, right? Let me know when you're ready to proceed."

"Sure. I'll do that."

The builder hopped into his white pickup emblazoned with Timber Framing Plus on its doors and drove down the lane.

Emma jammed her hands on her hips.

"Don't even start." Alexia glared back. "It's no big deal. Brent even said so."

"He said it was setting him back! Just pick something already!"

"I'm not like you. I have to mull."

"You've had forever to mull. This is like college all over again." Alexia had completed five years of college while jumping from track to track. Who knew what she wanted to be when she grew up? No one. Not even Alexia herself. So, it should be no surprise that she couldn't pick between grays, blues, greens, and tans. Sheesh.

"It's no skin off your back, *twinnie*."

Emma sighed. "True enough. I'm sorry." Not that she felt repentant, but what was the point? It wasn't Emma's problem, but man, everything her twin did reflected on Emma one way or another.

Reflected on the entire Cavanagh family. They'd had enough of the community's judgmental eyes on them with the discovery of Dad's indiscretion that resulted in the twins' half-sister showing up while they were in high school. Then Mom and Dad's separation and near divorce, the arson that sent the ranch house up in flames... no, Emma would be happy if Jewel Lake forgot the past. She would do everything she could to make the Cavanagh name something to be proud of again, like her older brothers were doing. The sisters' new business, Happy Trails Stables, would help.

Too bad Alexia didn't care about anyone but herself.

As for Vivienne, she was conscientious to a fault. Emma could count on her, but confide? Not so much.

Their brother Noah's farrier truck drove onto the property. Emma heaved a sigh of relief. Her favorite brother — don't tell the others — was exactly whom she needed right now.

Noah jumped out of the driver's seat. "Did I miss Brent? I thought I passed his truck on the road into town."

"Yes. He'll be back soon, though."

"Good. I want to finalize specs for the blacksmith shop." He opened the truck's backdoor, and his two golden retrievers tumbled out.

Noah's words faded away as Emma realized someone else exited the passenger side. A tall, dark, and handsome guy who looked vaguely familiar. Probably from her daydreams, because of course her fantasy boyfriend would match the romance-novel cliché.

"Hey, do you two remember Josh McDiarmid? He attended Creekside about the time you did."

Josh? Oh, Emma remembered him, all right. Her brain did acrobatics, trying to align the teenage jock with the gorgeous grown man beside Noah's truck.

"My sisters," Noah continued, pointing them out in turn. "Alexia and Emma."

Older by eight minutes, Lex always got to be first.

Alexia's smile widened as her eyebrows tipped up. "Seriously? You're Joshy?"

"Hey, Lex. Good to see you again." He doffed his cowboy hat and held it as he shifted from one boot to the other.

Right. He'd always had a crush on Alexia, never noticing Emma. In turn, Lex had liked Danny, who'd liked Shelby. No one had ever figured out that Emma had crushed on Josh, part of an entire chain of unrequited teenage puppy love she would rather forget.

Josh glanced at Emma. "Hi, Emma. It's been a long time, hasn't it?"

"Sure has. Nice to see you again. You're working with Noah?" One of Noah's dogs, Deidre, nudged Emma's hand, and she stroked her ears.

Josh nodded. "Noah's been teaching me to shoe horses."

Noah reached over and squeezed the younger guy's arm. "He's barely strong enough to wield a smithy hammer. I'm getting him in shape. When I'm finished with him, he'll be tough enough to wrangle a mustang."

That bicep looked plenty developed to Emma, straining against the sleeve of Josh's T-shirt.

"Ooh, muscles." Alexia batted her eyes at Josh.

His face flushed, and he looked down.

Humility became him. It certainly wasn't ever found on Alexia.

"Mind if I show Josh around Happy Trails? He'll be working out of this shop more than I will, but don't worry.

I'll be overseeing his work until I'm sure he's fully capable."

Alexia grinned. "He looks capable of anything."

Great. This would rewind Alexia's clock back by six-plus years. She was already reverting to the teen who'd treated boys as a game. Maybe she'd never stopped.

If Emma hadn't been watching Josh so closely, she might have missed the pleased smirk that swept his face at Alexia's words.

"So, tell me what all is going on here." Josh swept his hand to include the entire site.

"Noah didn't tell you?" Alexia sounded surprised.

"A bit. But I'd like to hear your vision directly."

That should shut Lex up. She didn't have a vision.

Emma stepped a little closer, but not too close. "We're setting up a boarding stable and riding academy. You can see the bones of the stable already. The indoor arena will be over there." She pointed. "We've got a few corrals built and a makeshift shelter for our horses." Emma had spent enough years during college without her mare at the ready.

Josh nodded thoughtfully. "Jewel Lake needs something like this."

"We thought so. We did a lot of market research in setting up our business plan." At least she and Viv had. Dad had required that before sinking cash into their idea.

"Living quarters onsite?" Josh asked.

Emma pointed back down the lane. "You may have noticed a spur road down a bit. Timber Framing Plus is building three houses off of that. Those are top priority." Something Lex hadn't quite figured out yet.

"Looks like you've got a great plan in place." Josh might

have been speaking to Emma, but his gaze lingered on Alexia.

Some things never changed.

Wow, Alexia Cavanagh had become a more beautiful woman than the cute teen girl had hinted at.

Josh had known he'd run into the sisters when he took the job with Noah's farrier service. Or, at least, he'd hoped so. Last he'd heard, they were away at college. Emma had been going for her teaching degree, but he couldn't remember what Alexia's major had been. Not that it mattered. He'd find out later.

Would there be a later? He remembered the angst he'd felt as a teen when he'd asked Lex out and she'd turned him down. She'd had such a crush on Josh's buddy that Danny had been frantic to become invisible. What Josh wouldn't have given to be the object of her affection back then!

Probably just as well, though. They'd only been kids.

That had been then. Now, it seemed they were both still single. A sign? Maybe. Only time would tell if she were the woman for him, but Josh intended to find out. He'd been all but tongue-tied around her in high school, and it seemed old habits died hard.

Emma, ever polite, kept the conversation going and answered his questions about the business they were building here.

He remembered her, too, of course. She'd been the

quieter one, the studious twin, the one their class voted most likely to succeed. He turned to her now. "I hear you're a teacher?"

Emma smiled at him, her face lighting up. "Yes! I've just completed my first year at Creekside teaching middle-school history and English Lit. It's part-time for now, but that's working out well, since it means I'll still be able to pull my weight around here."

She didn't have a lot of weight to pull. She'd always been slightly smaller than her twin. Like Alexia, the adult version of Emma looked pretty great.

Josh's gaze drifted back to Alexia. She definitely had the edge, as she always had.

Emma's smile didn't look quite as bright when he turned back to her. Whatever that was about.

Noah coughed. "The smithy will be over here."

Right, Josh wasn't onsite to speculate about the past or the future. He was here as an employee of the twins' brother, which might put them out of his league. The Cavanaghs had money. If anyone doubted that, then just look at their parents buying land and building houses for their daughters.

His own dad and stepmom barely kept a roof over their own heads, let alone Josh's or his sister's. Josh didn't need them to anymore. He was ready to work for his living. Noah had done well with his farrier business. He'd even had a circuit through western Montana for years before giving up most of his distant clients to focus on Jewel Lake and to work on the family ranch.

But some of those former clients had kept in touch and still wanted a farrier who came right to their premises to care for their horses' hooves onsite. And so, Noah had hired Josh and trained him. For all Noah's teasing, Josh had worked with him long enough now that there wasn't much he couldn't handle. Including the circuit they'd been building back up.

Now, Josh looked at the foundation with a pad-mounted transformer beside it. He'd seen the architect's sketch, so he had something to go on besides a slab of concrete. "Hard to believe the contractor will have this ready for business in a little over a month."

Noah laughed. "I know, right? He's got a lot of brands in the fire here, building my sisters' houses and the stable and everything. What's the timeline on the houses, Em?"

Josh didn't miss the glare Emma sent to Alexia before she answered.

"End of summer, at least for mine and Viv's. Who knows about Lex's."

Noah grinned and elbowed Alexia. "What's the holdup?"

She shrugged. "I can't make up my mind which way to take the design. I don't love any of the options."

Emma opened her mouth. Closed it again. Pinched her lips tight.

Huh. Looked like friction in the sisterhood.

"Where's Viv?" Noah asked.

"At the clinic," Alexia answered. "Where else?"

Josh didn't know the third Cavanagh sister well. She hadn't been part of the family until they'd all been in high school, and she was two years older than him and the twins. They'd never run in the same circles.

"I'll check in with her later."

Josh tried to wrap his brain around the fact that these contemporaries of his had parents who offered them land and a business and houses on a silver platter. At 16, with a crush on Alexia, he hadn't understood the differences between their families. Was he reading too much into it, even now? Only one way to find out.

Noah's cell rang, and he stepped aside to take a call.

Josh looked between the twin sisters, then focused on Alexia, shot a quick prayer heavenward, and braced himself. "Hey, Lex. There's a great sounding concert in Missoula on the weekend. Would you like to go with me? We can catch dinner and..."

Her eyes widened as though in disbelief.

Not the reaction he'd been going for.

"I, um, I don't know. I'm pretty sure I'm busy this weekend."

He managed a smile. "Short notice. I get it. Maybe some other time."

By the look on her face, maybe not, but Josh wasn't the timid teen he'd been way back when she'd first rejected him. He was a nice guy, a Christian, a steady worker, and she'd come around to seeing those qualities in him. He'd jumped the gun; that was all. Unless she cared about his lack of prospects?

But he had a decent job with her brother. If being a farrier was good enough for a Cavanagh, it should be good enough for *dating* a Cavanagh. He could be patient. He'd be working from the blacksmith shop right here at Happy Trails, possibly for years to come. He had nothing but time.

Patience. Right.

Never Josh's strong suit.

CHAPTER

Two

J osh and Noah wandered over to the site of the future blacksmith shop, consulting a sheaf of papers as they talked to each other.

Emma turned to her sister. "You were rude to Josh." Also rude to Brent, but at his age, he could handle himself. He must be at least 40.

Alexia gave her a stink-eye. "I was not rude. Who just asks a girl out they haven't seen for six years? He doesn't even know who I am anymore."

Join the club. Emma didn't know who her twin was, either. "Dinner and a concert aren't the same as a marriage proposal. A first date is for getting to know someone a little better. Besides, Josh always had a crush on you."

"I'd rather not rehash high school, thank you very much." Alexia dusted her hands together. "Hey, I thought we were going for a ride up the back trail."

"But Brent said he'd be back, and Noah and Josh are here..."

"None of them need us for anything. C'mon."

If this was the only thing the twins had in common anymore, Emma was all in. "Just a sec."

She strolled over to the smithy as she heard Alexia striding away. "We're going for a ride, unless you need anything."

Noah glanced over. "No, we're good. I texted Brent, and he'll be back in about half an hour. Josh and I are going to do some site prep while we wait. Take the dogs?"

Emma allowed a peek at Josh, but he nodded at Noah.

"Okay." She turned away, whistling for Barney and Deidre, who bounded in front of her. "Have fun."

"You, too." But it sounded like her brother had already tuned her out.

Josh had never tuned her in.

Gah! Why did that feeling of inadequacy always creep in and swamp her? She'd aced college. She and Alexia had shared very few classes, but Emma had beat her twin out every single time, and her GPA was a full point higher. She wasn't second best just because she was second born.

Except with guys.

Josh, specifically.

She'd gone six full years hardly thinking of him unless she ran into his grandmother at the church office. Mrs. McDiarmid must be nearing retirement — she'd been a fixture there forever.

Emma found Alexia by the horse shelter, slinging a saddle over her mare's back. Emma reached into the storage trailer and grabbed Desiree's tack. It didn't take long before they'd mounted.

Alexia pointed up the scant path with a question in her eyes, and Emma nodded.

They'd have to develop these trails better before they started offering beginner lessons. At the very least, they needed one well-maintained loop that could easily be ridden in 20-30 minutes, like the most popular loop at Sweet River Ranch, where Emma had worked summers during college.

She'd learned a lot about cooking for a crowd from the resort's chef, Nadine, but the older woman had made the kitchen a fun environment. Emma had made some good friends up there.

Tina and Eryn had been a lot easier to get along with than Alexia.

Why, again, was she going into business with her sisters?

Right, Dad had pulled her aside and asked her to. Reminded her that Alexia and Vivienne both needed security, needed purpose, needed family.

Emma couldn't say no to her parents. Not when she remembered the depression Mom had languished in before Vivienne's appearance, which had jolted Mom into leaving Dad for a while and taking the twins with her. Those months in a cramped apartment in town had marked Emma's teen years. Attending Creekside Academy instead of being homeschooled at Rockstead, the family ranch, had broadened her horizons immeasurably and awakened a desire to become a teacher herself.

But Vivienne's arrival had deepened the rift between Emma and Alexia that had already started to form. Alexia had all but shunned Emma as she turned her efforts to being Viv's new best friend. The twins' relationship had never quite recovered.

Emma studied her sister's back as Alexia rode in front of her up the path, Noah's dogs ranging ahead. Yeah, there were a lot of things they couldn't talk about. College, friends — guys, apparently — and even their faith. At least, Emma was pretty sure Alexia still believed in God. If not, she wasn't sure she wanted to know.

Lord, please help me to reach my twin. I miss her friendship, and she seems so aimless and lost. Please draw her closer to You — draw both of us, please. Help me know how to be her friend.

The path opened into a meadow filled with wildflowers that reminded Emma of a spot on Rockstead, though that vista held a peek toward Glacier National Park on clear days, and this one didn't. She hollered at Alexia. "Wanna make daisy chains?"

Alexia turned in her saddle and laughed. She reined in her mare and swung off. Like all Rockstead horses, Domino had been trained to remain in place with the reins dropped on the ground. Ground-tied, their brother Travis called it.

Emma slid off Desiree, whose tail and ears twitched as she took in the surroundings.

"Remember making these for Mom when we were kids?" Alexia twined two stems together.

"She said she prized them more than the diamonds Dad gave her."

Alexia's laugh sounded bitter. "Little did we know she actually meant that. It wasn't just a line to boost our childish egos."

"But they're happy together now."

Grinning contentedly, the dogs flopped into the tall grass.

14

"That doesn't change all those years they weren't. When Mom lived in her basement rooms, and they hardly ever interacted."

"I know. I remember."

"How do you just get over that kind of trauma?"

Emma shot her twin a glance. "Are we talking about ourselves, or about Mom?"

Alexia jerked to her feet and flung the few flowers she'd looped together as though they were a baseball. "Anyone. They ripped our entire foundation from under us."

"But you said it yourself. They weren't happy. Mom was depressed. Dad was angry." Emma shuddered to remember his rages.

"People shouldn't have kids."

Emma laughed. But maybe her twin wasn't joking. "Why do you say that?"

"Because kids have no say in anything. They don't get to pick their parents. They don't get to decide if their families are any good or not. It's like a slot machine, except kids don't even get to spin it. They get to live with whatever random results there are. And just like gambling, the odds of winning are in the negatives somewhere."

At least Emma didn't have to worry about her sister acquiring a gambling addiction. But she still needed to take Alexia's outburst seriously. "So, you plan to never have kids?"

"You got it."

"Look at our nieces and nephews. They have good parents. Our brothers are awesome dads. There are other decent men out there." Probably. Emma had watched the Sullivan grandsons find love over the past few years up at

Sweet River as well. She'd never been tempted to throw her hat in the ring to win one of them, but that didn't mean they weren't great guys. And now, those who were fathers seemed to excel at that, as well.

Alexia snorted. "Many of those kids had a rough start. Look at Toby. Travis and Dakota swapped him back and forth every weekend for years. And Gavin didn't even know his dad until he was, what, eight? And Bella—"

"You're right. We live in a sinful world, but Jesus came to redeem us and redeem our relationships."

"Of course." Alexia reached for Domino's reins. "Let's ride."

After the builder's return, Josh listened as he and Noah discussed the electrical needs of the smithy. While Noah's farrier business owned a mobile forge to tow behind his truck, Happy Trails Stables would house a permanent installation similar to the one up at Rockstead Ranch. This location would be more easily accessible to residents of Jewel Lake than the one at the ranch, and also to horse owners toward Missoula.

He'd get to oversee this smithy, so he should be paying better attention, but he kept listening for the clop-clop of horses' hooves. Would the sisters return before Noah and Brent's meeting disbanded?

Alexia had shut him down, but he'd been too hasty. They hadn't seen each other in years. She might not be wearing a ring, but that didn't mean she wasn't dating someone. Noah hadn't said anything about any of his sisters having a significant other, but it could be a newer relationship. Also, why would Noah confide that information to Josh?

No, she'd said she thought she was busy. She hadn't said she already had a date. It had been a clear brush-off.

He didn't want to take it that way, though. He'd be seeing a lot of all three sisters working here at their riding stable once everything was fully functional. He shouldn't have jumped in like that. He'd bide his time before asking again and make sure she'd warmed up to him. Apparently enthusing over his muscles wasn't the same thing as wanting to date him.

Point taken.

But the game wasn't over.

"I've been focusing my crew on the houses," Brent said. "I have another crew finishing up a convention center in Priest Lake. They'll be here next week to focus on the smithy then the stable."

"I'd like to see what's going on with the houses." Noah gestured toward the spur road Emma had mentioned.

"Sure. Let's drive over, and I'll walk you through."

Josh felt like a kid tagging along as he hopped back in Noah's truck, and they drove the short distance to the cul-de-sac. Three beautiful timber-frame houses were arrayed around the circular end.

The structures were clad in white house wrap, with windows still wearing manufacturers' stickers. Hammers rang out as a crew of three nailed asphalt shingles onto one of the roofs. The guys were shirtless and tanned, even though it was only the end of June.

Those guys had muscles, too. Was Alexia an equal-opportunity admirer?

He sighed. Probably. But he wouldn't give up.

"This one is Emma's." Brent pointed to the left. "Your dad said to focus on hers first, since she has the summer off from teaching to help with painting and such. She's also been on the ball to select materials." Brent pointed to the middle structure. "That will be Alexia's. Looks like it will be last to be completed." He pointed to the third. "And Vivienne's. She's got a decent rental in town, Declan says, and she's very busy at the medical clinic, so she won't be around as much for hands-on help. Still, she's seemed eager in the couple of meetings she's been able to make."

Declan was the twins' dad. Oh, and Noah's, too. The brusque rancher had terrified young Josh but seemed a decent enough man now.

"Yeah, Lex is having some issues," Noah replied casually.

Wasn't that gossip? Also, what kind of issues?

"She'll come around, though," Noah went on. "Once she figures out what she wants, nothing much is going to stop her."

Brent chuckled. "Well, I'm waiting for that moment with her house. It's at lock-up with the layout determined, but beyond that, I've got little to go on. But there's plenty to keep us busy around the property while she figures things out. She's got a few weeks to decide before it sets back my crew."

That was the Alexia Josh remembered. Easygoing until

she fixated on something. Sadly, as teens, she'd never fixated on him. She'd had eyes only for Danny.

Danny's family didn't even live in Jewel Lake anymore. Last Josh had heard, his friend worked on a ranch over by Saddle Springs. Danny was no longer in competition for Alexia's heart.

Joshua McDiarmid had been raised in the church. He was a God-fearing, praying man. He'd pray for an opportunity to show Alexia Cavanagh how good they could be together.

CHAPTER

Three

L ook what someone dumped by the road." Noah's voice sounded harsh and unforgiving as he held out his denim shirt, the pouch it formed wiggling.

Emma peered into the nest to see three tiny kittens, their mouths open in a near silent mewing. "Aww. Where's their mama?"

"That's what I'd like to know. More than that, I'd like to know what poor excuse for humans would dump babies out in the wild."

"Like those abandoned pups you found a few years ago."

"Yeah, just like that, except I found that litter way up the mountain. Clearly, they weren't meant to survive. At least, these were left near town."

Emma reached into the shirt and plucked out a calico. The kitten rooted around in her hands. "It's hungry. What do I feed them?"

Noah's eyebrows tipped up. "Are you going to be responsible for them?"

"Of course. What's a riding stable without barn cats? I'd

planned to wait until we were settled, but God thought otherwise." She nuzzled the ball of fluff against her cheek.

"Good solution. I'll take them home if you don't want them."

"Of course you would, but I've got it. Look, there's even three, one for each of us."

Noah stared at her.

"Right, I have no idea if my sisters want cats or not. Viv probably doesn't. A cat might leave germs around her house. And who knows with Lex. I'll take them all in that case."

Her big brother slung his arm over her shoulders and squeezed her. "Good job, Em. You won't regret it."

"I guess I should call the vet's office to see what to feed them? Unless you know and just aren't telling me."

"Call the vet. They seem pretty young. They might need formula for a bit. I don't know cats so much."

Even now, Barney and Deidre were sniffing at the squirming creatures in Noah's shirt, but they weren't aggressive in their curiosity.

"Okay, leave them with me. I'll make the call." Emma took the shirt and carried it into the shade, where she sat cross-legged on the ground with the nest in her lap. She pulled out her phone as both dogs flopped beside her. Silly things. They seem to have decided the kittens were their charges.

The vet's office invited her to bring the kittens in right away for a quick checkup and food, so Emma pulled to her feet again. "I'm headed into town with them," she called to Noah.

"See you in a bit." He waved.

"Hey, where's Josh today?"

"Coming later. Why, did you miss him?"

Cheeky big brother. "He's your constant sidekick. Of course, I noticed his absence."

"Uh huh." Noah winked. "I'll tell him you asked."

She rolled her eyes as casually as she could manage. "You do that."

Noah laughed and turned back to the smithy. In the two weeks since their earlier meeting, Brent's crew had erected the timber framing that formed the small building. Noah now cladded the outside with rustic-looking boards.

Emma tucked the kitten bundle into the passenger seat of her pickup and headed into town. She soon found the kittens appeared to be in good health. She returned to the property with a supply of formula, kitten food, a portable enclosure, a litter box, a pet carrier, and a cozy bed. She'd get toys and a scratching post on her next trip.

Now, where would she set these babies up? She wasn't living onsite yet, but she didn't really want to transport them and all their gear to Rockstead and back every day, either.

She'd no sooner pulled to a stop near the group of partially completed buildings than Josh approached her truck.

He opened her door and grinned. "I hear you're a kitten mom now."

Who knew all it took was infant mammals to make him notice her? "Seems so." She exited the vehicle as he stood back. Then she reached into the backseat and pulled out the carrier. "Here they are."

Josh leaned closer. "They look healthy, if tiny."

"That's what the vet said. Probably about four weeks old. I guess I should be thankful their owner didn't dump them as newborns."

"Who does stuff like that, anyway?"

"I know, right?" Emma shot a glance at Josh, who actually looked at her for once. "Anyway, Happy Trails is their new home. I wish I didn't have to haul them to and from Rockstead every day, but I won't be able to move into my house for a couple of months yet, and none of the other buildings are finished enough to protect them, either. I wouldn't want a bear or mountain lion or someone's stray dog to attack them if I just leave them here all night unattended."

"Oh, no. Of course, you can't leave them. You're commuting from the ranch?"

"Sure am. There's progress here every day, and I'm excited to see it happen. I just can't stay away."

"Why not set up a travel trailer or some sort of RV? We've got power to the site."

She stared at him. "I hadn't thought about that, but I'd hate to buy one for such a short time."

Josh bit his lip. "My brother-in-law broke his leg, so they won't be camping in theirs for at least a couple of months, and by then it will be fall. Want me to see if they're open to you borrowing or renting it?"

"You'd do that for me?"

"Sure. Why not?"

"Because I thought you never even noticed me. Just my sister." Ouch. That had been pathetic.

His chuckle sounded self-conscious. "I noticed you! And Alexia doesn't care about me, anyway. Unless maybe she does, and she's just playing hard to get?"

Emma snorted, perhaps not the most ladylike sound. "Who, Lex? Never." Also, maybe she should have cut the sarcasm from her voice.

"Could you... could you find out? I'd really like to date her. What would it take for her to see me in that light?"

Emma gulped an immense amount of air. This was a new one. If Alexia wanted to date Josh, absolutely nothing in the universe would stop her from pursuing him. Therefore, she didn't find him attractive.

And it killed Emma to realize that Josh really didn't see her, after all. He'd come to the truck to see the kittens only so he could probe her about her twin. How to make a girl feel second-best. Second place didn't get the trophy, and it didn't get the guy.

"You care for Alexia that much? You don't even know who she is now. High school is way back in the rearview mirror."

"I know." He scuffed the toe of his cowboy boot in the dirt. "But old feelings die hard, and I'd like to find out if there's anything there." He gave Emma a chagrined chuckle. "I know it's kind of a long shot."

What an understatement. "Yeah, it is."

"Has she told you how she feels about me?"

"No." That might only be because Emma hadn't asked. She didn't want to know.

"Can you put in a good word for me?"

This sounded so middle school, where hormonal kids' interests were passed around in semi-private gossip sessions. Emma might have only been teaching tweens for the past year, but she'd overheard her share of who liked whom. Plus, she had a memory.

"I can, but I can't guarantee you'll like the results."

"I know." Josh met her gaze with his deep brown eyes.

And Emma felt like she'd do anything at all to have his attention, even for a little while.

"Hey, Josh! I didn't expect to see you tonight. Did I forget I was supposed to go to work?"

Josh had been watching his nephews on the evenings his sister, Tammy, served at the Golden Grill. It drove Ian crazy that he wasn't even able to care for their kids without help.

"Nope. I actually stopped by because I knew you weren't running off somewhere."

"Ah... okay. Joining us for dinner?"

He hesitated. "Sure. Why not?"

"I'm not that bad a cook." Tammy laughed. "The boys will be happy to see you. All they can talk about is the fun they have with you. You're their favorite uncle."

Josh laughed. "Their only local uncle."

"That, too," his sister said with a laugh before lowering her voice. "Maybe you can cheer Ian up. He's had a rough day."

"Aw, I'm sorry to hear that." Josh set his cowboy hat on a shelf. Ian usually managed to keep the worst of his pain from Tammy. It must be bad today if she'd noticed it.

Two preschoolers barreled into the room, and he knelt to grab his giggling nephews. "Hey, you two. Are you being good for your mommy?"

Soren nodded. "I'm always good."

Two-year-old Blaine chortled and took off, checking over his shoulder to see if Josh was following. The monkey.

"They miss Ian roughhousing with them. If you run off some of their energy, I'll call you squared up for a free dinner."

"Sounds good. Where's Ian? I need to talk to both of you."

Tammy shook her head with a sigh. "I should have known you had an ulterior motive." She led the way into the living room. "Look who's here, honey."

Ian lay on the sofa with his casted leg elevated. "Hey, Josh."

Josh gripped his brother-in-law's hand. "How's it going?"

Ian grimaced. "I've definitely been better."

Tammy perched on the arm of the sofa. "What's your question, or do you need to warm up to the topic first? I need to pay attention to dinner pretty quick."

"Smells like meatloaf?" Yeah, Josh was stalling.

"Yep. Baked potatoes and green beans." She tumbled her hands. "Talk."

Josh chuckled. His sister had usurped all the family's decisiveness. "You know I'm working for Noah Cavanagh and he's building a farrier shop at Happy Trails, right?"

Ian frowned. "Happy Trails?"

"The new boarding stable and riding academy the Cavanaghs are building on the perimeter of Agate Bay."

"Right. I remember you mentioning it now."

"Emma Cavanagh needs temporary living quarters onsite while her house is being built." Josh still couldn't wrap his mind around Declan sinking this kind of money into setting his daughters up for the future. "I thought of your travel trailer, since I doubt you guys will be using it much this summer."

Ian flinched and closed his eyes. "Don't remind me."

Tammy squeezed her husband's shoulder. "We could talk about renting it to her. You're right that we're mostly homebound for a while."

"Thanks."

"Don't thank me yet. Ian and I will discuss it and get back to you."

"That's fair."

Tammy hustled from the room just as Blaine stretched his arms for Josh to pick him up.

"Emma Cavanagh, huh?" Ian asked. "Thought it was the other twin you had a crush on."

Josh waved his hand in dismissal. "Ancient history." Then he tickled the toddler for distraction.

"Are they single?"

"Seems so."

"Well, you might get another chance, then." Ian frowned. "Wasn't there a third sister?"

"Yes, Vivienne. She wasn't raised at Rockstead. Didn't even know who the Cavanaghs were until everything came out after her mother died."

Ian adjusted the pillow under his leg. "Sounds rough."

"Yeah. I haven't run into her much. She's a nurse practitioner working at the clinic downtown."

"Dr. Loewen's office?"

"I think that's the one." Josh eyed his brother-in-law. "Anything I can do for you while I'm here?"

"I don't think there's much anyone can do. This stupid knee is going to take as long as it's going to take, and it's going to hurt as much as it's going to hurt."

"Meds aren't strong enough?"

"I hate taking the big ones. I hate feeling so woozy and out of it."

"But if you need them..."

"I don't."

Blaine wiggled to get down. Guess Josh hadn't been paying the kid enough attention.

"Does your doctor know the meds aren't cutting it?"

Ian sliced his hand. "Doesn't matter."

Josh would beg to differ, but he didn't plan to force painkillers down a grown man's throat.

"I don't know what we'd do without you, Josh. You're already working full time and still here a lot of evenings to cover while Tammy works. It's killing me to be a lump on this stupid sofa. Can't do anything worthwhile it seems."

"I'm sorry, man. And I'm happy to help." Was it stretching Josh? Absolutely. His days were full, but Tammy and Ian were hurting financially with all the bills and little income, so it was the least he could do. "I'll take them to the playground after dinner."

"Thanks. And Josh?"

"Yeah?"

"This here leg is a pain in the butt, but I'll tell you one thing."

"Hmm?"

"I wouldn't want to suffer through this without my wife at my side. You need a woman, Josh. You're what, 24?"

"Just turned 25." While Ian had been in the hospital, actually.

"Find the right girl and marry her. I'd never quite figured out what a helpmeet was before that log smashed my knee and leg. I was always the strong one, taking care of everything. Well, guess what? Your sister is tougher than I thought, and I need her strength."

"Maybe I should just avoid falling logs until I find my partner." Josh tried to imagine Alexia doting on him like Tammy cared for Ian. Failed.

Ian rolled his eyes. "Sure, as if you can run your own life."

"Too true. God's in control."

"Wish He would have dropped that tree a few seconds later or a few feet over."

"I get it, man. I do."

"Dinner's ready!" Tammy called. "Josh, want to grab the boys' plates and put them on their little table in the living room?"

"Sure."

Ian struggled to pull himself into a sitting position, and Josh shoved an extra pillow behind the man's back before going to help Tammy.

His sister turned to him with a worried look. "Do you think he's okay?"

She wasn't looking for vague reassurances. "He might need his prescription looked at."

"Yeah. He refuses."

"Other than that, I think he's doing as well as can be expected."

"Quit talking about me!" Ian hollered from the other room.

Josh laughed and grabbed his nephews' plates. "Looks good, sis. Thanks for feeding me."

CHAPTER
Four

A w, they're so sweet." Vivienne smoothed the top of one tiny kitten head with the tip of her finger.

"You can hold it, you know." Emma picked up one of the others, and a purr rumbled through the kitten.

"I'm headed to the clinic soon. I don't want to have to change again."

Emma bit off her words. How could anyone deny the worth of snuggling a tiny mammal for even a few minutes? But then, Vivienne hadn't been raised on the ranch with all the puppies, kittens, calves, and colts. Emma and Alexia had hauled baby chicks around, too.

Their half-sister had been born and raised in Spokane, never knowing their dad, neglected by her mother, and mostly cared for by her older sister. There hadn't been a lot of nurturing. Emma's parents might have had their own sets of issues — multiple sets — but growing up on Rockstead with six older brothers had provided a foundation for the twins that Vivienne had never dreamed of.

"Do you want one of these for your own?" Emma asked.

Viv gave her a startled look. "What do you mean? I thought you were thinking of barn cats that belonged to Happy Trails as a whole. Creatures to keep the rodents down."

"They can be pets, as well."

"I can't really see having an indoor cat. Maybe a small dog like your mom's? But not even that. I'll be working long hours between the two jobs."

Emma had called it. "We'll want a dog or two, as well. Too bad Noah had Deidre fixed. Golden retrievers would be perfect for a public place like this. I'll have to scour the local shelters and see what comes up."

"Not until we're settled, right? I can't believe you took on these kittens with everything so up in the air."

Emma raised her chin. "Should Noah and I have left them to die?"

"Of course not, but that's what shelters are for."

"Well, I'm not going to take them there. I prefer to think of their abandonment here as serendipitous. They're meant to be ours." Or Emma's, at least.

"What does Alexia say?"

"Oh, she thinks they're the cutest things ever." Truth… but then she'd walked away and forgotten all about them.

"There you go." Viv checked her watch. "I need to wash my hands and get going."

"Are you planning to cut back your hours at the clinic once we're fully operational?"

Viv raised her eyebrows. "I went to school for eight years, Emma. I'm not giving up my hard-earned independence."

"That's not what I meant. Cutting back isn't the same as walking away."

"Are you giving your notice at the academy?"

"I'm only part-time, and I won't seek more hours if we can make a go of this."

"If? I didn't know failure was an option."

"It's not an option if we work together, all three of us. We need to be all in." Something Emma thought had happened, but these days, it seemed she was the only one who cared enough to see it through.

"I'm in. You know I am. But this—" Viv waved her arm around "—isn't everything to me."

"It's not everything to me, either."

Viv's eyebrows tipped up.

Was Emma the only one who saw things clearly? "Jesus is first. Our whole family comes next. This boarding stable is only a means to an end."

"Of course, Jesus is first. I didn't mean to imply otherwise."

"I know." She did know, right?

One of the Timber Framing Plus trucks jounced into the cul-de-sac and came to a stop in front of Emma's house. Several young men surged out.

"Who's that?" Vivienne's voice was low and urgent.

"Which one?"

"The driver."

Emma shook her head as she hollered an enthusiastic hello to the work crew. Some of them waved back. "That's the contractor's son, Finnley Callahan."

"He's cute."

"Seems nice, too, from what I've seen."

Finn approached the sisters. "Good morning." His gaze bounced between them, settling on Vivienne.

"Hi, Finn. I'm not sure you've met my sister Vivienne. You've been working on her house the past few days." Emma pointed at the structure across the way.

"Nice to meet you, Vivienne." He turned to Emma. "Any further instructions this morning?"

"No, I think you've got the latest."

"All right then." He nodded and turned away.

When he'd rejoined the crew, Viv jabbed Emma with her elbow. "He's been working on my house?"

A frustrated scream roiled up Emma's throat, but she managed to choke it off. "He's been moving from place to place along with the rest of Brent's crew."

Viv's gaze lingered on the young builder as the group began to offload materials from their cargo trailer.

"I thought you were in a hurry to get down to the clinic."

"Right." Viv blinked and dusted her hands together. "I am. Will you be here all day?"

"I need to stop by the academy for a couple of hours this afternoon but, otherwise, yeah."

"Take care of those kittens."

"I am. I will."

Vivienne hopped into her hybrid car and cruised away. Did she glance back at the men?

Emma shook her head. Alexia was toying with Josh, and now Vivienne nursed an attraction to their contractor's son. Emma might be the only sane one in the bunch.

The Timber Framing Plus crew consisted mostly of 20-something guys. They were probably nice, but they weren't from around here. They were based in Galena Landing in northern Idaho, and they built structures all around the Inland Northwest.

Emma's roots were solidly in Jewel Lake, and since she wasn't moving away from this property her dad had bought for his daughters, there was no point in speculating on any of those cute workers.

On the other hand, Josh might be a guy she could fall for... if only he weren't fixated on Alexia.

A kitten mewed in her arms as the three of them rooted around. First order of business? Getting the trio fed and settled. After that? She still had to fulfill the promise she'd made to Josh. To find out Alexia's true feelings and report back.

Not that she needed to ask, because her twin's response seemed clear enough. Was it just that Emma could read Alexia? Not the same thing as words she could parrot to Josh, though. When she told him Alexia had clearly stated disinterest, would he see Emma?

Not that she wanted to be a consolation prize.

But maybe it would be worth it.

A few construction workers were offloading materials from a cargo trailer when Josh drove into the cul-de-sac and leaned out his window.

"Have you seen Emma this morning?"

One of the guys turned toward his truck. "She's in there." He pointed at the house on the left.

Those guys had been working miracles since Josh had been here a week before. Then the place had been full of drywall dust, but now it smelled like fresh air... and paint.

"Emma?" he called out as he stepped into the foyer.

"Hello?" She came into his line of sight carrying a paint-brush. "Oh! Hi, Josh."

Emma wore a white coverall streaked with green paint and a conductor's hat on her head. All her long, blond hair must somehow be piled inside it.

He'd never have guessed a woman dressed this way could look so adorable. Also, she had a streak of paint on her nose. Should he point it out? Wipe it away himself?

None of the above. He looked down at the plywood subfloor but couldn't help noticing her red sneakers had paint smudges, too.

Enough. He focused back on her eyes. Only her eyes. "I shouldn't have gotten your hopes up about my sister's travel trailer. It looks like they're selling it, so borrowing it won't be an option after all."

A moue of disappointment crossed her face. "That's fair. Thanks for checking."

"I feel badly. I shouldn't have said anything until I talked to Tammy and Ian." How could he have guessed, though? He knew things were financially tough for them, but he hadn't realized they needed to liquidate some of their assets to help make up the shortfall.

"It's okay. Really. There would have been no need to ask her if I hadn't agreed it sounded like a good idea."

"The whole chicken and egg dilemma." Josh chuckled ruefully, shaking his head.

"Yep. It's often hard to know which should come first. Anyway, you made me no promises, so it's all good."

"Thanks for understanding." Josh gestured around the open living area to his right. "This is coming together nicely."

Emma beamed. "I'm pleased. I picked a green palette for my place." She pointed into the bathroom behind her. "Brent said the cabinets and tiles might be a while yet, but I could go ahead and paint."

"Green, huh? I would have pegged you as a pink girl."

She tipped up her eyebrows. "Do I seem so much like a girly-girl?

Did she? He'd seen her ride her horse like a wild thing, hair streaming behind her. Not so girly... but still feminine. Josh held up both hands in self-defence. "I plead the Fifth."

Emma's laughter rippled around the room.

She had a nice laugh.

So did her twin. Josh cleared his throat. "Have you had a chance to talk to Alexia yet?" It had been a few days, after all.

Emma closed her eyes for a second before looking back at him. "I haven't. We've both been pretty busy lately, and we've barely crossed paths."

"Oh. Okay." Josh managed to keep his face impassive. He'd followed through with what he'd promised Emma. Why couldn't she have done the same? Of course, both requests had been his idea. Had she seemed reluctant to talk to her twin? If so, he hadn't noticed. Anyway, why would she?

He was overthinking this, as usual.

"Josh? I haven't forgotten."

"Okay. Good." He forced a smile. "So, uh, I shouldn't keep you any longer. Wet paint edges drying out and all."

Her hazel eyes widened. "You're right! I'd forgotten about that. I did a little painting when my parents rebuilt after the fire, but that's been years. I'm out of practice."

"Noah's waiting for me, or I'd offer to help." He even meant it.

"That's nice of you."

"Well, have fun. Talk to you later." He turned on his heel and made his way back across the foyer.

This house might not be a whole lot bigger than the one his dad and stepmom had owned when he was a kid, but the vaulted ceilings with huge beams visible made it seem much grander. And this domicile was only for one person.

Of course, Emma probably expected to have a family one day, as her sisters most likely did, too. It made sense for each of them to have their own home from the start.

Money wasn't a problem for Declan Cavanagh. This whole setup was probably a graduation gift to his daughters.

Josh's dad had signed over the family's 15-year-old clunker to Josh and bought himself something a few years newer. As for college? There'd been no money for that. If it hadn't been for Grandma's perks from working in the church office for decades, Josh and his sister would have been educated in public school instead of Creekside Academy.

He eyed Alexia's two-story house next door as he hopped into his truck. Why, again, did he wish to pursue her? He wasn't in her league. He knew that. Looking at these houses only made it clear.

Alexia hadn't seemed snooty in high school, just disinterested. Danny's family had been little better off than Josh's, and she'd focused on him like a laser beam. Not that kids understood the vast difference money made. No, those realities were the realm of adults trying to find their own place.

He'd hold onto hope until or unless Alexia made it clear otherwise. She'd be honest with her sister, right? She'd tell Emma if she'd only been distracted the other day. Maybe she'd really had plans and hadn't intended to sound so dismissive.

Josh had surprised her. End of story. She probably regretted turning him down.

He drove toward the smithy.

Wow, look who was full of himself today. He was nothing to her. Hadn't been. Wasn't now. Wouldn't ever be. He should circle back and tell Emma not to bother. He should simply face the facts and be satisfied with his lot in life.

Just because he'd turned a quarter of a century old didn't mean he needed to find his life partner any minute soon. Plenty of guys his age were still single. It would be fine.

Tell yourself that all day long, McDiarmid. It's fine.

W here've you been lately?" Emma looked up from her spot on the floor in the cabin she and her twin shared at Rockstead. The kittens clambered all over her lap.

Alexia stretched both arms over her head. "Hanging out with Trinity Kennedy. You know her?"

Emma frowned, trying to remember. "The blind potter?"

"That's her, only she's not completely blind. Just mostly."

"I've seen her and her husband around at church. Dale owns Communication Location downtown, right?"

Alexia nodded. "Him and his brother."

"How did you get to be friends with Trinity?" Wasn't the woman something like ten years older than her and Lex?

"I thought I might like to be a potter, and she offered to show me what the job is like."

Emma blinked. Swallowed. "You want to be a potter." Just last week Lex had been enthused about silversmithing.

"I said I was thinking about it." Alexia's chin came up.

At least it explained why she was rarely around the build site. "Have you picked a color palette for your house yet?"

"What's it to you?"

Emma bit back a retort. Took another deep breath. "You'd be a lot closer to Trinity's studio if you were living at Happy Trails."

"It will be months before we're moved in, anyway."

"Yeah, and you'll have gone through five more potential career interests by then."

Lex glared. "Just because you think you have your life together doesn't mean everyone aspires to the same boredom you're in for with a life of teaching middle-school English. I can't imagine anything more monotonous."

"Why don't you tell me how you really feel?"

"Just did." Alexia smirked then lowered herself to the floor and plucked one of the kittens out of Emma's lap. "These are the cutest."

"They are." Emma might prefer an apology, but she'd settle for a change of subject. "Only a few more days of bottle feeding, and I can put them straight onto kitten food."

"Nice." Lex nuzzled the orange and white kitten against her cheek. "This one is Blaze."

Emma had already chosen names, but she could give her twin this win. "Suits him with that coloring."

Lex tapped on the calico's head. "This one is Trouble." The kitten grappled with Alexia's finger like a boxer.

"I call her Tangle. She wrestles with the toys like it's a full-contact sport."

"Tangle. I can live with that. What about the tortie?"

"I've been calling her Coonie."

"Coonie?" Alexia frowned. "What kind of name is that?"

"If you heard her chittering, you'd know. She sounds just like a baby raccoon."

"Huh. Also, are you sure about their genders?"

Emma shook her head. "Not completely, but most calicoes and torties are female, so it's a safe guess."

"Didn't know that."

"Education has its uses."

"Don't even start." Alexia rolled her eyes. "So, are you tired of green yet?"

Change of subject again. Alrighty then. "If you mean the color palette of my house, nope. I chose a few different shades for different areas, and I'll use other colors for pops here and there."

"Let me guess. Hunter green for a pop."

"Hunter isn't another color, in case you didn't know." Her twin didn't rise to the bait. "I was thinking butter yellow. Maybe some pink and blue here and there. I found a floral duvet set with all those in it that really sets a tone I love."

"Cool." Alexia stroked Blaze's back, and the kitten's rumbling purr grew in volume.

"The farrier shop is coming along well." Emma eyed her twin. "Noah and Josh have been onsite a lot."

"Oh, yeah?" Though Alexia's response didn't sound all that curious.

"You interested in Josh? You didn't really give him an answer the other day."

Alexia wrinkled her nose. "I told him I was busy. Isn't that an answer?"

"Sort of? But you made it sound as though you might be open another time."

"How blunt does a girl need to be? Do I need to march up to him and say, 'Joshua McDiarmid, I wouldn't date you if you were the last guy on earth. I don't find you the least bit attractive.'?"

Emma shouldn't have found her sister's words so energizing. "I guess then at least he'd know."

"Mom taught me to be nice."

"We can be honest at the same time as we're being nice."

"Whatever. He was immature and needy in high school, always hanging around Pastor Eli with hero worship in his eyes."

"I hate to remind you that we graduated six years ago. Maybe we were all immature then."

"I guess. I can tell you one thing, the boy has some muscles now he didn't have back then."

The *boy*? He was so much more. But Emma needed to tread carefully. "Muscles can be attractive."

"Sure." Alexia laughed. "What girl doesn't love her some brawn? But it's only part of the package."

Well, Emma had received the answer to Josh's question, loud and clear. Would she find it in herself to be quite as blunt as Alexia had been when she passed on the message? She cringed at the thought.

"I think he's got more going for him than muscles."

"You want him? Go for it."

If only it were that easy. "I just meant he seems like a nice guy." Who only had eyes for her sister. Emma tucked the tortoiseshell kitten into her cozy bed and pulled to her feet. "So, pottery, huh?"

"It's fun playing with mud."

Wow. And Alexia thought Josh remained juvenile. "What are you making?"

"So far I've wrecked everything I've tried."

Life lesson right there. *Keep your mouth zipped, Em.*

Alexia set the ginger in with the others. "What's for dinner?"

"I ate in town."

"Oh. Wish you'd have told me so I wouldn't have come all the way up here hungry."

"I'm sure there's stuff in the fridge, or go over to Mom and Dad's. I'm calling it a night."

Alexia's eyebrows rose. "At 8:30?"

"I plan on having a long soak in the tub with a good book, so if you need the facilities, now is the time."

"Sheesh. I don't know why I even bothered coming home."

Good question. Why had she? Once the two of them had been so close, but that had been before Mom walked out on Dad, accepted a teaching position, and moved the twins with her to that dinky apartment. Once Alexia had more potential friends to choose from, she'd all but abandoned Emma. Vivienne had moved in soon after, and that had been the death knell to their once-tight unit.

Was starting a business together really a good idea, or would it backfire?

Josh had noticed Alexia's pickup parked outside Bayside Kiln for the past couple of days on his way to Happy Trails. Was she working for Trinity Kennedy? Maybe packing product for shipping to the galleries that sold their unique designs?

Hey, if she liked that sort of thing, he'd buy her a piece. Oh! A vase from Bayside filled with a bouquet from Petals. Just something casual and pretty, like Alexia. He made it happen then tucked the gift upright in a bucket on the floor of his truck on his way up to the stables.

Josh veered into the cul-de-sac. Yep, Emma's pickup was in front of her place, empty kayak racks on the roof. He grabbed the vase and strode up the dirt walkway to the open doorway. He stepped inside. "Emma?"

She came around the corner from the bedroom wing, and her eyes lit up at the sight of the flowers. Just as quickly, her jaw firmed as she looked at Josh. Whatever that was about. "Hey."

"I'm wondering..." Maybe this was a bad idea, but he was committed. Should he have bought two? Or maybe even three? But he hadn't, and this one already had a card on it with Alexia's name.

"Yeah?" She leaned against the wall, arms crossed.

"Would you mind giving these to Alexia for me? Maybe

don't tell her who they're from unless she seems open to the idea."

Her gaze flicked to the flowers and back to his face. "We talked last night."

"Oh?" Josh couldn't keep the single word from sounding hopeful. "What did she say?"

"I really don't think she's interested, Josh. Sorry."

"I mean… did she say that?"

Emma nodded.

"In so many words?"

She straightened. "Josh, she's not interested, okay? Sorry to be the bearer of bad news."

Oof. Way to wound a guy's pride. "Can you give these to her anyway? I bought them for her."

"Sure. Why not?" But Emma's voice didn't sound upbeat at all.

"Are you okay?"

"You know I teach middle school, right?"

He blinked. Where was she going with this? "Yes?"

"This smacks of tweens, and I think it's a bad idea. She turned down your offer of a date, Josh. I asked her if she might be interested some other time, and she seemed pretty clear that she wasn't. I'd like to not be in the middle of this."

Josh flinched. Emma was right. He was being stupid. Also, he shouldn't have involved her. Why did talking to Alexia tie his tongue in knots? Why couldn't he take no for an answer?

Also, what now with the bouquet in his hands? "One last try?"

"Josh."

"You're right. I know you are. But I already bought it."

"Go find her, and give it to her yourself."

"I think... I think she's busy."

"Aren't we all?"

"Right." He braced himself. "And I need to be at work in like five minutes. I don't have time to track her down, and these will be dead by the end of the day if I leave them in the truck."

"Uh huh."

"Can I leave them here regardless? You can offer them to your sister... or you can just enjoy them. Your call. But they may as well not go to waste."

"I don't want them here, Josh. There will be workmen in and out all day."

He looked at the cheerful flowers. Yellow sunflowers. Pink snapdragons. Stems of lavender. "Please?"

"Whatever. Stick them in a corner somewhere." Emma turned away.

Josh heard her sneakers on the plywood subfloor as she disappeared around the corner. There was a bit of a nook beside the front door. He could tuck the vase there. Emma hadn't said what the contractor's plans were for today, so maybe they would be out of the way.

At the very least, he didn't have a better idea. He set the vase down, straightened the blue checked bow, and headed toward his truck.

"Hey, is Emma in there?"

Josh turned to see a guy about his own age coming toward him, a tool belt slung low on his hips. "Yes."

"Great. We've got hardwood for her. I know she'll want to double check the boxes before we offload everything." The guy grinned and jogged into the house. "Hey, Em!"

Didn't that seem a little personal for a construction worker? Josh glowered at the guy's back for probably two minutes too long then climbed into his truck.

Emma and the workman came out of the house together. She was laughing. The guy grinned at her.

Josh growled. She'd been nothing but grumpy with him.

She said you were acting like a tween.

Had he been?

Maybe?

The workman levered the door of the cargo trailer open and offered Emma his hand to step inside.

She didn't need help. This girl could spring onto the back of a horse already in motion.

Yet, she took the guy's hand and smiled at him.

Josh wasn't jealous. What a ridiculous thought. He was interested in her twin sister, not her. Uh… why was he still sitting in his truck watching her?

Emma jumped out of the cargo trailer and seemed to notice him for the first time. Like maybe she thought he'd already driven away.

Well, he hadn't, though he had no idea why not. He turned the key in the ignition, put his truck in gear, and reversed around the cargo trailer before zooming toward the smithy leaving a poof of dust in his wake.

It wasn't so thick that he couldn't see her in his rearview mirror as she put her hand on the workman's arm and looked up at him.

Aargh. Josh had zero intention of noticing Emma. He wasn't going to. Nope.

CHAPTER
Six

T hat was fun. We should do it more often." Vivienne slid off her mare and stretched from side to side.

"We should." Emma managed to hold back her 'I told you so,' but she'd been thinking it. "We need to get the rest of our trails laid out this summer."

"Things are just so busy, you know?"

For Viv, maybe. Alexia seemed to be looking for make-work projects anywhere besides at Happy Trails. Thankfully, Emma was still on summer break for a few more weeks. Riding Desiree gave her shoulders a good break from painting the walls in her new house. Who knew how long it would take one person? Her sister-in-law Dafne had offered to come help. Maybe Emma should try to drum up a painting party to finish the job.

Emma led Desiree into the stable, Lex and Viv right behind her. The building was structurally finished with space for 20 horses. Maybe she could leave the kittens' carrier in the tack room now? No. What if she were detained getting away from Rockstead one morning and the trio was locked in too long? She couldn't risk it.

Alexia began removing Domino's tack. "I thought we might get a better view of Maranatha Inn along the path, but there's only that glimpse from the top."

"I'd wondered about that, too," Viv replied. "Their acres of Christmas trees give them a buffer zone. I guess that's nice for them."

"It's good for us, too." Emma released Desiree's cinch strap. "There shouldn't be any complaints about smelly horses or loud riders this way."

"I suppose." Alexia sounded thoughtful. Wonders never ceased. "The lookout would be a good place to build a picnic shelter or gazebo, don't you think?"

"Huh. I never thought of that."

"I have my uses."

"Never said you didn't. But that's a good idea."

"How can we haul all the materials up there?" Vivienne asked. "The trail is too steep for a wagon."

Emma shrugged. "We can hire someone like Jude Kline from Sweet River Ranch. He can drop loads from his helicopter."

"Won't that be expensive?" Vivienne gave her head a shake. "Never mind."

Right, Viv hadn't grown up with their father. She didn't know that Dad would never have spent an extra penny until the last half dozen years. He'd been a lot less stingy since coming to Christ.

"It's worth looking into." Alexia looked over at Emma.

"Can you ask for Jude's rates? Then we can figure out if it's doable."

Emma raised her eyebrows. "How about you price out materials then?"

"Sure. Why not?"

Huh. So, Alexia cooperates when it's her idea.

Noted. Emma glanced at her watch as she curried Desiree's coat. "The pizza should be here in ten."

"Good idea on pre-ordering. I'm starved." Viv fed a piece of carrot to Nightingale. "Besides, I can't wait to see how much you've gotten accomplished since I last saw your place."

Emma heard Alexia's muffled snort, but she wouldn't dignify that with acknowledgment. "It's coming along. Yours is ready to paint now, isn't it?"

"That's what Brent said. We've picked all the colors for the various rooms. Unlike you, I'm hiring it done. I just don't have time."

"It's a lot more work than I thought it would be."

Vivienne exited Nightingale's stall and paused in front of Domino's, where Alexia poured a measure of grain for her mare. "How is your place coming, Lex?"

"I still don't know what I want."

Emma couldn't help meeting Vivienne's eyes and noting her older sister's concern. But there was no point in saying anything. The schedule was between Alexia and the contractor. If anyone needed to intervene, it would be Dad. Emma was done being her sister's keeper. For now, anyway.

The three of them made their way to what Emma had started to think of as Sisters Close. Wouldn't that make a great name for their little street, since close was just another name for cul-de-sac?

"Come on in." She swept the door wide, barely missing the bouquet still sitting on the floor behind it. "Oops."

"Ooh, pretty." Alexia had spied the flowers. "Isn't that vase from Bayside Kiln? I think I recognize Trinity's work."

"I believe so. Viv—"

"Don't you have a better place to keep it?"

"Not yet, I don't."

Lex crouched down to admire the flowers. "Who's it from? Do you have a secret admirer?"

As if. Emma waited, aware of Viv's gaze bouncing between the twins.

Alexia's eyes widened as she looked up, the little card in her hand. "It's for me?" She turned it over. "Who's it from? You?"

"If it were from me, I'd have simply given it to you."

"Of course." Alexia frowned then gave an awkward chuckle. "So, it's *me* who has a secret admirer?"

"I bet it's one of those cute workmen," Vivienne put in.

"You think?" Alexia rose to her feet, leaving the vase where it sat.

Because there truly was no table or counter on which to set it.

"That lavender smells great." Viv bent to sniff.

Emma had been enjoying the fragrance when the odor of paint didn't overpower it.

"Lavender." Alexia tapped her chin. "Also a pretty color. What do you think of doing a purple palette in my place?"

"It's not one of the options Brent gave us." Vivienne rose with a frown.

Alexia shrugged. "He gave a starter list. I can't imagine anything more drab than gray, beige, green, or blue. Sorry, guys, but it's true."

"So, you don't like my walls?" Emma's eyebrows shot up.

"They're okay. You know we've never liked the same stuff."

Truer words had never been spoken. Take Josh, for example, not that Emma would utter his name in present company.

"Well, *I* like them." Vivienne stood beside Emma as though her sister needed her support.

"I do, too, and that's all that counts."

An engine sounded outside, and Emma breathed a sigh of relief. "Sounds like the pizza is here. I'll grab it."

Josh had been a wee bit intimidated by Noah Cavanagh, but add in the other five brothers, and he wished he could crawl into a hole. Adam was a former rodeo champ, for crying out loud. Travis took no prisoners. Nathaniel, Noah's twin, might be soft-spoken, but that didn't translate to pushover. Blake turned everything into a joke. And the youngest, Ryder, was the face of Rockstead. All Josh needed was for Declan—

And the final truck turned into the Happy Trails yard. Great.

Josh put his back into helping shift the forge, anvil, and

other equipment into the smithy, which didn't take long with so many strong and willing hands.

"I haven't been down here for a while." Declan hopped out of his truck and looked around. "The stables look finished."

"Emma says there is still a lot of interior work to do in the offices and tack rooms," Noah told his dad.

Declan studied Noah. "Are the other girls pulling their weight?"

Noah held up both hands as though in self-defense. "Getting involved in that is crossing trade lines. My job is right here." He thumbed at the smithy with its double doors wide open.

Josh understood, though. He'd been here on and off for several weeks, and he'd seen Emma at least ten times for every single view of Alexia or Vivienne. It helped that she was on summer break from teaching, but where was Alexia?

The truth had been slow to sink in. He hadn't seen her truck at Bayside lately when he'd driven past, but she hadn't been at Happy Trails, either.

Short answer: she was avoiding him.

She hadn't thanked him for the flowers. He hadn't signed them, but wouldn't she have guessed? Wouldn't Emma have told her, even though Josh had asked her not to? Maybe Emma had kept the flowers for herself and thrown out the card.

He kind of doubted that by how frustrated she'd looked the day he'd dropped them off. She'd basically called him immature.

That stung.

"Do you have a horse, boy?"

Josh blinked and looked at Declan, who stood right in front of him. "Uh, no, sir. I don't."

"Once we get a few head down here, I want you to feel free to do some riding on any of them. You'll want to get to know their personalities, anyway. Won't that make shoeing them easier?"

"That's true, sir." Something about the older man's direct, piercing gaze brought those *sirs* out of Josh's mouth like nobody's business. "I'd be honored."

"You'll be working out of this shop, right? So, if you decide to buy your own horse, we'll make room for it here. Least we can do."

Likely Alexia wouldn't view it the same way. "Thank you. I'll keep that in mind."

"Noah says you're experimenting with other areas of blacksmithing?"

"Yes. Not a lot, so far." He hadn't had a ton of spare hours since Ian's accident. "I've forged some decorative leaves with hooks for hanging hats or towels. That sort of thing."

"Do you have any here that I can see?"

Josh hesitated. "It's been on my own time, sir."

Declan shrugged. "That wasn't why I asked. Besides, how you and Noah work things out isn't any of my business."

"I have a few hooks in my truck. I planned to drop them off at my grandmother's house later. It's her birthday tomorrow."

"May I see?"

Why was the man so curious? But Josh nodded and

strode over to his pickup to retrieve the objects. Hopefully the man wouldn't notice the bits of baby's breath and sprig of lavender languishing in the footwell.

If Declan noticed, he didn't mention it. He took the hook out of Josh's hand and turned it over a few times before handing it back. "Nice work. I'm a fan of aspen trees, myself."

Josh's chest puffed with pride. "They're one of my favorites, and I'm glad the leaf is recognizable."

"I might get you to make a set for Kathryn, if you can fit it in. Or an entire coatrack with a bunch of hooks. Maybe four feet long? Two levels of hooks?"

Josh blinked. "I can sketch something up for you, sir."

"You do that." Declan clapped him on the shoulder. "We've been happy with your work shoeing the Rockstead horses, but don't neglect your other talents."

"Thank you, sir." Noah had taught him the basics of being a farrier at the family ranch, but he'd taken over that aspect again as Josh gained experience to service a wider area.

If Josh had his way, he'd do more decorative work and less driving the farrier circuit. They'd limited time away to a few days every six weeks, but they might have to cut that short with him watching his nephews several nights a week.

But Josh was thankful to Noah for an excellent job he could do independently. He could meet people, which was sometimes a disadvantage, but so long as they talked about horses, it wasn't so bad.

Buy his own horse and keep it at Happy Trails? He'd never considered that. Raised a townie with little extra spending money, he'd just been thankful to ride with whichever friends invited him over, like Danny used to do.

His own horse. Huh. The idea took root, but it wouldn't come to fruition anytime soon. The Cavanagh sisters had their mares onsite now, but Happy Trails wasn't set up for boarding yet.

Declan had turned to his sons. "Let's go over to the girls' places and see the progress since we were last here. Josh, you might as well come, too."

"That's okay. I'll stay here and unbox the tools and supplies. We've got timber shelves built, ready for them." He really didn't want to see any of the sisters. Didn't want to notice where the flowers had ended up.

Worst case scenario might be if they were at Vivienne's place because both twins had rejected his overture.

He doubted they'd be at Alexia's. Last he heard, the place was full of drywall dust, which would be a bad environment for delicate blossoms.

What had he been thinking?

He hadn't been. It had been an impulsive act, and one Emma had correctly pegged as juvenile.

Josh needed to do better. Maybe he needed to set aside his dreams of dating Alexia and look around Creekside Fellowship's College and Careers group again. Josh hadn't been to college, but he wasn't the average age anymore, either.

A bunch of men from church met one night a week for a study. Monday, wasn't it? Noah had invited him twice, but he'd declined. He had little in common with all those married men. Besides that, several group members were

Noah's brothers. Where were the young working guys without a significant other?

The Cavanagh men joked and laughed as they made their way to the trio of houses, leaving Josh to set up the tool shop.

He'd volunteered, after all.

CHAPTER

Seven

"What did Brent say about your color scheme?" Emma asked Alexia. Her twin didn't drop by her house often.

Alexia shrugged. "He seemed fine with it. He gave me a fan deck from the paint store and told me to pick up to four colors then mark which goes in each room."

Emma nodded. "Yeah, he did the same with me. Are you going to do the painting yourself?"

Her twin gave her a horrified look. "Are you kidding me? I've seen how many days you've been at it here and how many times you've had a bubble bath to soothe your muscles. Not a chance for me. I'm with Viv on this one. Dad's got oodles of money. He doesn't need me to save more for him."

How could Emma explain the sense of satisfaction she'd found knowing she'd done as much work as she could on her home? "What's the schedule?"

"The paint subcontractor is doing Viv's this week. Then

they have another project before they can come back for mine. I have lots of time to finalize the choices."

Emma bit down on her tongue. Even with doing the work herself, she was way ahead. It had been nice of Brent to show her how to tape off walls and use the sprayer, though. It had certainly speeded things up.

Alexia crossed to the windows flanking the fireplace in the great room. "I see you kept the flowers."

"You didn't take them." Emma had created a makeshift table out of two sawhorses and a scrap of leftover plywood. The bouquet certainly cheered up the dusty corner.

"You never told me who they were from."

"That's true."

Alexia turned and studied her. "Josh McDiarmid, right?"

Emma reacted a hair too slow to fool her sister. Not that she wanted to lie.

"I'm right. Grr. Why can't that guy take a hint? I've given him more than a hint. You wonder why I've been scarce around here? I don't want to keep running into him and his puppy-dog eyes. It's creepy."

"It's not like he's a stalker or anything. I don't think he means to be creepy."

Alexia rolled her eyes. "I wish he didn't work for Noah. I wish Noah'd had the courtesy to ask us what we thought of Josh taking over the smithy on *our* property. It's no skin off Noah's back, but it makes a big difference to the vibe around here."

"You didn't see it coming when Noah started talking about offering shoeing services here when he already has a forge at Rockstead and a mobile unit?"

"Why should I have?"

"He'd mentioned hiring Josh not long before. To me, it seemed like a natural progression of events. Why would Noah keep driving all the way down from the ranch when Josh lives five minutes from here?"

"You know where Josh lives?"

Heat shot up Emma's face. "I know where his parents live. Same place they always did."

"Josh could live anywhere. He's not a kid."

Nice of Alexia to finally notice. "Okay, fine. I've seen the farrier truck parked at Emerald Estates where Pastor Eli used to live. I realize it might be coincidence, but it seems reasonable that's where Josh lives."

"You haven't asked him?"

"Why would I?"

Alexia shrugged and turned back to the flowers. "Maybe I'll take these to match up paint swatches. It's a pretty color combo, don't you think?"

A keen sense of loss jabbed at Emma's gut. "The pastels do go together nicely. The florist did a great job."

Her twin studied her for a minute before seeming to accept the answer at face value. "Do you think Brent would care if I chose four completely different colors instead of four shades of the same one? Yellow in the kitchen and dining room. Lavender in the living room and master." Lex tapped her jaw. "Maybe pink in the other bedrooms. Or blue. Oh, wait. I like green, too. When it's not all over everything like in here."

"You'd have to ask him, but I don't see why he'd care. That sounds pretty."

"You think?"

"Yeah, I do." In fact, why hadn't Emma thought of using

multiple colors herself? "I've heard pink or peach tones are best in bathrooms."

"Which is why you painted both of yours green."

"Yeah, well. The rooms both have decent windows, and I'm using daylight bulbs. It will be fine."

"It's got to be better than Vivienne's. Just the thought of all that gray makes my head turn foggy to match. Ugh."

Emma's thoughts exactly. "She likes it."

"She likes it *now*. Just wait until she has to live with it."

"She spent years in decrepit beige apartments with her mom. I agree that gray is an improvement."

"But the sky's the limit! She could have anything she dreams of. In fact, I'm going to live dangerously and ask Brent for *five* colors. I'll do pink *and* blue bedrooms and use green in the upstairs hallway."

Emma blinked. Wow, now that her twin had a direction, look at her go. Given her current expansive mood, the next thing Emma knew, Alexia would decide dating Josh might be a good idea, too.

And she didn't want to think about why that thought soured her gut.

"Hold her steady." Josh lifted Desiree's left hind foot and examined the shoe. "Hmm."

He tried not to notice Emma standing inches away, holding her mare's reins. Emma's skinny jeans were tucked into a gently scuffed pair of Tony Lama boots. If he looked up a little further, he'd see her yellow Happy Trails T-shirt tucked into those jeans behind a narrow belt. No looking up, though. He'd be checking out her backside, and the thought of *that* made a flush creep up his cheeks.

Not that she didn't have a nice backside. She had curves in all the places a woman should have them. So did her sisters. Like Alexia. He should be thinking about Alexia, the woman he wanted to date. Who didn't want to date him.

No, he should focus on Desiree's hoof. Emma had mentioned her mare seemed to be limping. One nail had a little play. He'd need to remove the entire shoe, clean up the area and check for bruising before replacing it.

"What are you finding?"

Josh grasped the first nail with his puller. "One nail is loose. Not sure if that gave room for a pebble or not until I get a closer look."

Why was he getting just as much of a whiff of Emma as he was of Desiree? Focus. He bent closer to the hoof, removed the other nails, then brushed the bottom of the sole. Ah, he'd found the problem. He used a hoof pick to remove the small stone wedged in the frog area. "There we go."

Desiree's tail swished, and Emma chuckled. "Where are we going?"

Out? But no. This was Emma, remember? "Found the problem. Not sure if the pebble caused the nail to loosen, or if the loose nail allowed room for the pebble. I'll spritz on this antimicrobial spray to prevent infection before I redo the shoe."

"Okay. Should I be giving her hoof baths?"

"Might be a good idea for a few days until it fully heals. She'll need to rest, too."

"I figured as much. We need to get our trails better developed. There's a lot of loose material up there. I hadn't realized how damaging it could be."

"Yep." He applied the spray and gently turned Desiree's hoof to make sure there were no other visible problems. Looked good, though. "Ready? I'll nail the shoe back on. It still looks in good shape."

"Ready."

He could hear her crooning to Desiree as he bent to the task. Finally, he set the hoof back down and ran his hand down the mare's hock. "Good. We'll give her a minute before I check her other shoes."

It would give him a chance to stretch his back, too. And to see Emma from a better angle. Not better, exactly. Just more conducive to talking instead of ogling. Not that he wanted to ogle her, but he was a guy, and she was a girl, and she stood right there.

Still no excuse.

Josh rose to his feet and slid his hand over Desiree's back. "Good job, girl. You'll feel better now."

"She will." Emma flashed a grin at him. "Thanks for seeing her with zero notice."

"No problem. The Happy Trails horses are my first responsibility, and there's only the three of them right now. Have all of you been riding up the same trails?"

"I've gone more than the others." Emma scrunched up her face. Adorable. "But yes, both Nightingale and Domino have been there, too."

"I should check all of them."

"Do you need a hand?"

Josh hesitated. "Not really, but it would go faster. Not that speed is everything." Maybe he just wanted to spend a little more time with Emma.

He liked Alexia, remember? But why, if she kept pushing him away? And did he like her for who she was... or who he hoped she'd become? Had liking her become a comfortable habit?

His gaze caught on Emma's for a moment. This was crazy. "I'll check her right hind foot next." He kept his hand on the horse's rump as he rounded her to make sure she stayed aware of his proximity. Then he crouched down, lifted the foot, and used the brush to expose the hollow. He examined the nails and tested the adhesion of the shoe. "This one looks solid. It should last until the next shoeing in a few weeks."

"Sounds good."

He examined the mare's front foot then exchanged places with Emma for better access to the fourth. Yes, he breathed a little deeper as he brushed past. She smelled a whole lot better than horseflesh... not that he minded the equine aroma. "Just that one pebble caused all her problems. She should do all right now."

"One little thing, huh? Isn't that exactly like life?"

Josh blinked and looked at Emma. "Waxing philosophical over a lame horse?"

"She's not lame." Emma cradled Desiree's head in her arms and rested her cheek against the mare's. "That sore foot is nothing a little pampering won't cure, right, baby?"

"Uh, yeah." Josh should not be feeling jealous of a horse. Besides, he liked Alexia. The reminder seemed to come from a distant voice, as though it tried to convince himself of something he knew to be untrue.

Did he know that, though? He shook his head and took a step back. "Let me grab a few tools, and let's go see the others. You go ahead so I can see if Desiree's gait has improved any." He didn't want to walk beside Emma. Did that mean he wanted to walk behind her and observe her? Ugh. There was no good answer to any of this.

Emma led Desiree across the parking area to the corral next to the stable where the other two mares stood in the shade swishing their tails.

It didn't take long to examine the others. Whew. There was no sign of stuck pebbles or other problem areas on either of them. Josh straightened and patted Nightingale's shoulder. "All good. I should get back to work."

He didn't feel like it, though. A slight breeze drifted through the shade in the corral. Noah had left a few of the original trees near the smithy, but their shade wasn't as thick or refreshing as here.

Emma hopped up to sit on the top rail. "What are you up to these days?"

"I'm headed to Canyon Crossing in Saddle Springs tomorrow. Noah has the contract as their farrier, so I go out there every few weeks for a couple of days."

"They're a boarding stable like we're aiming for, right?"

"Yes. It's a lot the same. The original owners sold it a few years ago, and the new owners kept Noah on. Which I guess is me, now. They don't seem to mind."

She tilted her head and studied him. "Why would they?"

"Well, they made the contract with your brother. They weren't looking for a substitute."

"But Noah trained you, and he thinks you're ready."

"Right. And I feel ready. It's just a big responsibility, you know?"

Emma chuckled. "Like the first time I stood in front of a classroom and realized it was completely up to me to teach these kids to love English literature?"

He laughed, too. "Probably similar. Part of taking our places as fully functional adults."

"I suppose that's true. I'm sure you'll do fine."

"Thanks. That means a lot."

And somehow, it did. Josh didn't want to think too hard or too long about why that might be.

CHAPTER
Eight

So, we really need to get the trails cleared and groomed," Emma finished. "When can we set aside a few days to do that?"

Vivienne put up both hands. "I'm working a lot."

Emma stifled a flare of frustration. "But we all agreed to share equally in Happy Trails. You know it will take all of us to run this place."

"I still have a job." Viv crossed her arms and stared at Emma. "You know that."

Alexia scoffed. "What I know is that you can't decide whether to trust Dad or not."

"What?" Vivienne whirled on Alexia. "What on earth are you talking about?"

"That's the way I see it." Alexia shrugged. "You're willing to accept Dad's money for land and a house, but you also feel like you need to do everything yourself. You can't have it both ways."

"That's not how it is."

Wasn't it, though? Emma's twin may have hit the

proverbial nail on the head. "That's kind of like accepting Christ's salvation and then still feeling like we have to do all the hard work ourselves to get to heaven."

Both sisters stared at Emma.

Alexia shook her head. "I'm not sure how you got from here to there. Not everything is a spiritual metaphor... or whatever you call it, English teacher. This is about Vivienne being a Cavanagh, not about her Christianity."

Emma needed to learn not to spout everything that crossed her mind, but why couldn't the others see the similarity? But maybe her thoughts didn't serve the basic conversation.

"Why don't we see if the family can make a day or two of it with us?" Alexia suggested. "Our brothers are big and strong. Their wives can help. Even the older kids. A work crew will make it go more quickly."

"Great idea. Travis already volunteered to bring the skid-steer down when we're ready, and Nathaniel knows a guy who can bring a truckload of dirt."

"The skid-steer can pack the trail, too, right? With the roller?" Alexia asked.

Emma nodded and eyed Vivienne. "When can you take a few days off?"

"I already told you."

Emma tipped up her eyebrows and crossed her arms. Her twin mirrored her position as they leaned shoulder-to-shoulder.

"Fine. I'll ask. But you guys should know..."

"Know what?" Honey all but dripped off Alexia's voice. "That you're not really committed to Happy Trails?"

Vivienne's shoulders slumped. "I am. You know I am. I did a ton of the work on the proposal."

More than Alexia had done, for sure. But why did Emma feel like she was the only one all in now? She had a job, too! Just because she was on summer break didn't mean she wouldn't be spending hours away once school went back in.

Hmm. "Is something wrong at work, Viv? Are they pressuring you?"

"Not really. I just feel so responsible."

Alexia rolled her eyes, and Emma managed not to jab her twin with her elbow. "I understand feeling responsible, but we need to figure out how to make this work. All of us, together. Or we might as well stop right now. Dad can probably subdivide the property to keep the houses and sell the rest of it. If we're not fully committed to Happy Trails, we should cut our losses now."

Both her sisters frantically shook their heads.

Emma choked back her exasperation. "If you guys want to keep it, we all have to put in the work."

"Hey, I'm in." Alexia put her hands on her hips.

"Are you? Because you're not even here half the time, and you don't have a job requiring your presence."

"I *said*, I'm in." Alexia glared at her. "Didn't I pick my paint colors?"

"That's for your *house*, Lex. How about the riding stable? How about the property? How about everything else?"

"You say it like you think you're the only one keeping everything afloat."

Um, yes? Hammer, meet nail. But maybe she didn't need to dignify that with a response.

Alexia raised her eyebrows at their older sister. "Now, Viv, on the other hand, has done diddly-squat around here."

"I *said* I'd ask for a few days off." Vivienne glared at Lex. "Both of you have made it abundantly clear that I'm not your favorite sister. I'm doing the best I can, okay?"

Emma managed a sharp laugh. "You're *Lex's* favorite sister. Today, I'm not sure I have one."

"Oh, give it up already." Alexia shook her head. "Do we have nothing better to do than squabble like pesky children? We're sisters. All of us. None of us chose each other, yet here we are."

Wow, Lex wasn't often the one trying to keep it together. Usually that fell on Emma, but today? Today she just wanted to cut her losses and move far from Jewel Lake where no one knew who the Cavanaghs were. Where no one watched and judged her based on her entire family. Especially her sisters.

She should have applied for a teaching job somewhere other than Creekside Academy. Not only was it her own alma mater, but both her mom and one sister-in-law taught there. Why couldn't they make Cavanagh a positive name in the area again?

Okay, fine, it was more respected than it had been when she and Lex were teens. When everything fell apart between their parents and Dad had to seek anger management counseling. He'd been so explosive the kids had learned to tiptoe around him as toddlers. The twins had avoided him as much as possible and moved to town with

Mom when the parents split. Not that Mom had given them an option.

Nothing like hanging their dirty laundry for all of Jewel Lake to see.

And yes, things were better now, so why did Emma still feel like eyes were watching and judging? Was her imagination *that* good? And also, did it matter what people thought?

No... but yes? Habits were hard to break, and did it need to be broken? Hadn't Paul exhorted the Philippian church to conduct themselves worthy of the Good News about Christ? Which, yeah, was about God's family, not Declan and Kathryn's. She got that.

"How did the trails get to be the top priority, anyway?" Vivienne asked. "I thought we were focusing on getting the stables ready for boarding so we could start earning back the investment before spending another big chunk."

"Desiree picked up a pebble and a loose shoe from back in the woods." Hadn't Emma explained this already? "Josh picked it out and reset the horseshoe. When people board their horses here, they'll want to ride the trails, so the trails need to be a safe place."

Alexia snickered.

"What?" Emma glared at her twin.

"So, you and Josh worked together all cozy over horseshoes."

"Yeah? What of it? He's a farrier, and he works right here. What was I supposed to do, phone Noah and insist he come down?"

"Oh, don't get so hot under the collar. I just think it's

funny that Josh is still crushing on me, and you're still crushing on him."

Vivienne's gaze bounced between them.

"I'm not crushing on him." Too bad Emma couldn't have made her voice sound more certain.

"I thought you weren't into lying."

"I'm not." Except now. But there was no freakin' way she'd admit anything of the sort to her twin.

Alexia grabbed her shoulders and leaned in, studying Emma's face. "I don't believe you."

"Believe whatever you want."

"Oh, I will." Alexia smirked. "I definitely will."

Josh opened the truck's tool chest and double-checked that he had everything stashed inside that he'd need on his excursion to Saddle Springs. Cutters? Check. Pullers? Check. Hoof rasps? Check. On he went through his list. It would never do to need a specific tool and find he'd left it in Jewel Lake.

Wow, it was hot, even with his cowboy hat shading his face. At least, he'd cool off once driving. He needed to remember to thank Noah for getting the air conditioning fixed in the work truck.

Back to his list. He had a spare bottle of propane and...

"Hey, Josh."

His head flicked up so quickly at Alexia's voice that his

neck might need an adjustment. "Alexia. Hi." Had she changed her mind about dating him?

Did he want her to have changed her mind?

No? Yes? He'd gone so many years thinking that if she just gave him a chance, she'd see how good they could be together. But maybe he'd been deluding himself.

"Thanks for the flowers. At least, I think they were from you. Emma wouldn't say."

Heat that had nothing to do with the blistering July afternoon crept up his neck. Hadn't he told Emma to keep it a secret? But maybe Alexia had asked her point-blank. He didn't want Emma to lie for him. "Uh, yeah. They were so pretty they made me think of you." He cringed at how sappy that came out.

"Thanks for the compliment, I guess. I've left them at Emma's since her house is much more finished than mine. They look great there." Her smile looked a little pained.

"Okay?" He shifted from one cowboy boot to the other.

"Listen." She took a step closer, her gaze still wary. "You're probably a great guy. I mean, I'm sure you are, but I really wish you'd stop trying to impress me or trying to get my attention."

Josh opened his mouth to respond. Couldn't think of anything to say. Closed it again.

"It's not going to happen, Josh. I'm sorry if that sounds blunt, but I need you to hear me."

"But..." This time he got a single word out. Still didn't know what to follow it with, though.

"There's no but. I'm absolutely certain I won't change my mind. I... there's no chemistry between us."

No chemistry? Then what had Josh been feeling for

years? Sure seemed like zing to him. His conscience niggled. Okay, maybe he'd been making it up. How on earth should he know? "I'm sorry if I've made things weird." That, at least, was true.

"I'm sure there's a wonderful girl out there who will feel the same about you as you feel about her. It's not me. I doubt I'll ever get married. I don't even want kids. I'll be my nieces' and nephews' favorite aunt. That's a worthy goal, right? And I've already been succeeding at that. I'm known as the fun one."

She blabbed so much she must be finding this conversation just as uncomfortable as he did. That made him feel a tiny bit better.

"I know!" She snapped her fingers. "A girl like my twin sister. I bet if you asked *her* out, she'd love to go."

Josh's mouth opened and closed. Again. He'd turned into a guppy. "Emma?"

"She's the only twin I have."

Well, yeah. He wasn't that dumb. Maybe he sounded like it, though.

"Emma's great, especially if you like the intellectual type. You're a reader, right? I think I remember that?"

He nodded dumbly. Louis L'Amour wasn't in the same category as Charles Dickens. They'd studied *A Tale of Two Cities* in high-school English. Emma had come alive. He'd been bored out of his skull. But yeah, they both liked to read.

"Emma's a lot like me, except nicer. You should give her a shot."

"I… uh…"

"Give it some thought. I'll leave you to whatever you

were doing." Alexia patted his arm and looked at his open tool chest. "Which was what?"

"Getting ready to head to Saddle Springs for a few days. I'm driving over tonight so I can start shoeing horses at first light, when it's still on the cool side."

"Think about what I said. But don't think about me."

Josh straightened his shoulders. "You're sure."

"Absolutely."

"Okay." He could take this like a man. Twenty-five counted as that. They'd graduated from Creekside Academy six years ago. Some of their peers were already married with kids.

"Are we okay? I don't want it to be weird."

"Yeah. We're good. I'm sorry if I made it that way."

She swept her hand to the side. "Water under the bridge, never to be seen again."

"Thanks." He wanted to ask her again if she was certain, but she'd already said it bluntly.

The problem? He should feel more crushed. Maybe, in his heart of hearts, he didn't believe her. Or maybe his heart was smarter than his head and had accepted Alexia's lack of interest long ago. Maybe it had already moved on.

Hadn't he wondered about his awareness of — he would *not* call it interest in — Emma earlier when he'd reshod Desiree? Had he been so stubborn about thinking he wanted Alexia he hadn't even noticed her twin?

But could Emma actually be interested?

Because all Josh needed was for both Cavanagh twins to reject him. Then he might have to tell Noah he couldn't run the farrier shop at Happy Trails.

But, really... Emma?

CHAPTER

Nine

"We don't see much of you around here anymore." Mom stood in the doorway of Emma's cabin at Rockstead.

Emma gave her mother a hug. "I know. Brent kindly lets me camp out in the house with the kittens, so long as I'm willing to move from room to room to stay out of his workers' way."

"You don't even have plumbing yet."

"That's been a bit of a problem." Emma chuckled. "But I haul buckets of water from the smithy, and Brent has a couple of port-a-potties onsite for the construction crew. It's been okay. I should have water in the house within the next couple of weeks."

Mom shook her head with a smile. "You have a more adventurous spirit than I ever had."

"Oh, I don't know. I'm not the one who married a man I barely knew and uprooted everything to move to his ranch." Maybe she shouldn't have said that.

"It worked out in the end. But you're right. It was a big

risk, and there for a while, it didn't seem like it would be worth it." Mom squeezed Emma tight. "But then we wouldn't have had you and Alexia, and that's impossible to imagine."

When her parents had married, they'd each had three sons. Their twin daughters had been born a couple of years later. And then Vivienne, searching for her bio dad, had shown up when the girls were in their teens.

Emma moved deeper into the space. "I'm pretty glad to be alive most days."

Mom settled on one of the two chairs pulled up to the tiny table. "But not every day?"

"You know how it is," Emma hedged.

"I do. How are things with your sisters?"

"How did you guess I was talking about them?" Emma let her eyes widen in feigned innocence.

Her mother laughed. "I may have met the three of you before. I have to say, I had my misgivings when you kids and your dad hatched the Happy Trails plan. You three are all so different I wasn't sure — I'm still not — about the wisdom of binding your lives together like this."

"I know. I've had my doubts, too. Sometimes, I feel like I'm the only one all in." Emma sucked in a deep breath and released it slowly. "Why do I feel so responsible for my sisters?"

"I wish I knew. You've always been the level-headed one. The conscientious one. I'm not sure how your dad and I instilled that in you but not your twin so much."

It hadn't been Dad forming Emma's personality. At least, not in a positive way. He'd been a walking thunder-cloud about to explode during all of her impressionable years. Living with her father was likely what had taught her to look over her shoulder and gauge the mood of everyone around her.

"Who knows with Lex?" Emma sighed. "Whenever I think I have her figured out, she surprises me."

"One of these days the cogs will align, and she'll find her purpose."

"Watch out, world!"

"You're right." Mom laughed. "Then we'd all better duck, because nothing will stop her. She's picked her paint and woodwork and all, though, right? Finally?"

"She has, and it will be really nice. The clear maple cabinets and floors and all will look great with her pastels."

"Did the contractor balk at so many colors?"

Emma shook her head. "Nothing much seems to faze Brent. He just asked a few questions for clarification, nodded, and pocketed her list. Came back the next day to say he'd ordered everything."

"And your floors are going in?"

"Yes! We unboxed some of the red alder this morning, and it's gorgeous against the green walls. The crew will start in the master bedroom so I can quit moving around the house soon."

"Any cute young workmen on the crew?" Mom batted her eyelashes.

"You know it!"

"And...?"

"I'm not interested in any of them. They're nice enough, Finnley and Xavier, especially. But they live in Idaho and travel for their work, and I'm tying myself to Jewel Lake. Which is just how I want it."

"This mama hen is happy to have all her chicks nearby, but if you need to spread your wings and fly, I'll survive."

Emma hugged her mother. "Nope. I'm committed now. I might have concerns about my sisters, though."

"Vivienne?"

"She's working a lot of hours. Alexia accused her of something interesting a few days ago."

"Oh?"

"She said Viv was willing to accept Dad's offer to buy the land and build her a house but still feels like she has to earn her own way."

"Hmm. Isn't she simply trying to be an adult and not a dependent?"

"Can she have it both ways?"

Mom shrugged. "You are having it both ways. So are all your brothers. The ranch provided the funds for their families' homes, too."

"Right. I get what you're saying, but it seems like Viv is building herself a safety net in case Dad's goes poof."

"And that's not good?"

She didn't get it. "To me, it's like accepting God's gift of salvation and then still feeling like we have to do all the hard work ourselves to get to heaven."

"Ah." Mom tapped her jaw. "I see what you're saying now. You think she's trying to earn your father's approval, even though she already has it."

"Sort of? She seemed all in during the planning stages. She might have been in Great Falls not Butte, but we texted constantly and shared an online document we both added to. Lex did, too, but not nearly as much. I really felt like Viv and I were on the same page. Now?

She seems withdrawn and way too busy to be part of Happy Trails. Meaning our trails are not as happy as they could be."

"Remember Viv's situation before she met our family. Her life had taught her to look out for herself, because no one else was going to. Maybe she's simply afraid to give up her autonomy."

"Huh. You might be right." That would take some thinking about.

"Thanks for sharing your concern. Your dad and I will keep praying for you girls, and if you think one of us talking to Viv would reassure her, let me know."

"Thanks."

"Meanwhile, I've got the littler grandkids for a few days so all the big people can play in the forest at your place."

"Even Gavin and Toby are coming to help! Oh, and Lex put out word in town, and people have been stopping by for two days volunteering to help. The lady who owns Maranatha Inn — what's her name again?"

"You mean Julia Cox?"

"Right. That's her. She and her staff are bringing down lunch for everyone on both workdays. And the guy Dad bought our property from, Monte Newman? He and his sister's family are coming to help. Also, some of the other neighbors and people from the church."

"Your dad mentioned Eli Bryson offered to be in charge of the build."

"I'm so relieved. I felt like we were fumbling around in the dark hoping for the best. I panicked that we had all these people offering to help with no idea how to accomplish the goals, but Pastor Eli has been on several work crews for the Jewel Lake Trails Society, so he really understands how it's done from the ground up."

"No pun intended."

Emma giggled. "Of course not."

"Makes me wish I were going to be there in the center of the action with all of you, but I also can't say no to a day with the youngsters."

"Like many things in life, we can't have it both ways."

Mom rose to her feet and slung her arm across Emma's shoulders. "Truer words never spoken."

"That's everything, then." Josh closed up his toolbox and snapped the padlock shut.

"I'm so glad you're still doing the farrier circuit." Noela Meadows, the 50-something owner of Canyon Crossing Stables, tucked her thumbs through the belt loops of her jeans.

"Noah feels it's important to keep it up, even though he's pretty busy at Rockstead Ranch himself."

She chuckled. "It's important to us. I don't know why Saddle Springs doesn't have local farrier service. Maybe you'd like to move here and set up shop?"

Josh shook his head. "Great offer, but no. We've built a second location on the outskirts of Jewel Lake that will facilitate more horses there."

"Lucky Jewel Lake."

"It's my home, and I'm stoked about the new smithy.

Word is spreading and we've got quite a few horses entered into rotation."

"Just remember to leave our slot in the calendar."

"For sure. It's nice to get out of town once in a while. But then it's always nice to be home again."

"You were saying the new facility is at a boarding stable like Canyon Crossing?"

"Similar. It will be operated by Noah's three sisters. They're building houses on the property and will soon open boarding facilities and equitation lessons."

"Will they have as large a trail network as we do here?"

"Not as many miles of them, no. They don't have as large a property. But the community is coming together to help build trails over the next couple of days." Josh glanced at the angle of the sun and tugged his hat lower on his brow.

"You'll be helping with that?"

"Sure will. They're my bosses' sisters, after all."

"I remember when those twins visited here years ago. What a handful."

Josh chuckled. "I bet. I knew them in high school, high-spirited fillies that they were."

"Ah... romantic inclinations?"

He shook his head but felt the flush mount on his cheeks. If Noela noticed, hopefully she'd think it was simply the heat of the July evening. "Nah. Not really."

"Well, you never know. Someday a pretty cowgirl will catch your eye." The horsewoman rocked back on her booted heels. "I should let you get on the road. You've got a couple of hours to drive."

"I do." Josh checked the locks and the hitch to the

mobile forge again before nodding at Noela. "See you in five weeks."

"Sounds good." She backed away.

He jumped into the cab, started the engine, and pulled out of Canyon Crossing. He drove through Saddle Springs, past the Hats Off Motel where he stayed while he worked there, then out on the open highway. He took a deep breath, released it, and cranked on some peppy praise music.

No drumbeat was pervasive enough to keep his mind occupied, though. He'd spent the entire westward drive mulling the Cavanagh twins, and they hadn't left his mind since. He'd see them both again in the morning. Granted, there'd be dozens of other people there from what his sister said. Tammy was leaving the boys with Grandma — since Ian couldn't care for them on his own right now — and coming to help.

Was Josh man enough to admit to Emma he'd been wrong about Alexia and wanted to take her out instead? Equally as important, would she believe him? He cringed to think how he's asked her to get a temperature reading on Alexia's feelings for him. He could hardly blame anyone but himself if Emma didn't believe his change of heart.

But therein lay the problem. *Had* he changed his tune? Or was he contemplating this because Alexia had suggested it, and he'd do anything she said?

Aargh.

He'd noticed Emma on his own before Alexia's suggestion. He'd noticed her on and off for quite a while, and certainly on the day he'd reshod her mare, but she likely didn't know that.

The big question? Had Alexia also spoken to Emma? If she had, then Emma would turn him down. Josh might not be the smartest guy in the world with regards to female psychology, but it didn't take a genius to realize that no woman wanted her sister's castoff foisted on her.

I don't like him that way, but you might. See if you can distract him from chasing me.

Yeah, that wouldn't go over well. It didn't paint him in a good light. Also, paint could only disguise what lay underneath. It didn't change anything beneath the perception.

Josh had been in Emma's house before she'd started painting the great room. The walls had been covered with stripes and smears of drywall mud in preparation for a smooth, fresh coat of color. He hadn't been back to see the final result.

Had he changed underneath? Had he really moved on from Alexia? Didn't that take longer than a few days? Maybe not, if it had only been out of habit that he'd clung to his old hope she'd finally notice him.

No, it was going to take longer for Emma to see him as someone other than the guy who'd chased her twin. If only he hadn't involved her in that! But he had.

They'd be building trails over the next few days. Maybe he could 'accidentally' find himself working near her. Maybe he could figure out how to be her friend first.

CHAPTER
Ten

Emma leaned closer to her sisters as they surveyed the crowd listening to Pastor Eli's instructions. "I'm so glad he volunteered."

"You and me both, sister," Alexia agreed fervently. "I can't believe this many people showed up to help. There are dozens of them."

"We're related to more than a full third of them ourselves." Emma laughed. She nudged Vivienne's ribs. She seemed very quiet today. "You okay?"

"Yeah. Sure. This... this makes it all feel very real. Like the community actually wants a riding center."

"You doubted it?" Emma tilted her eyebrows up. "We did all that market research, remember?"

Vivienne shot her a glare. "Of course, I remember, silly. But I wondered if maybe we were putting our own spin on the results. Seeing what we wanted to see."

That didn't even dignify a response, as hard as they'd worked to get replies to the surveys. Sure, the townspeople numbered in the thousands, and only about 40 were here in work boots, leather gloves, and sun hats. They carried pickaxes, shovels, and chainsaws, ready to clear the trails.

Pastor Eli assigned several people to each Cavanagh brother's crew, except for Travis. He'd brought the skid-steer down and was ready to use it wherever manual labor wouldn't do the trick.

Emma found herself assigned to Noah and Taryn's crew, along with Josh. She raised her eyes to heaven for a few seconds. *Really, God? You think this is funny?* But she nodded to the other group members, which included Josh's sister Tammy, Kirk Kennedy, their neighbor Monte Newman, and a couple of others. "Thanks so much for coming and helping out."

Tammy sidled closer. "I felt badly that we weren't able to loan you our travel trailer to stay in this summer when Josh asked."

"It worked out okay. Don't worry about it."

"We had to sell it. Things have been a bit tight since Ian's accident."

"His leg was crushed in a logging accident, right? How is his recovery going?"

Tammy shook her head. "Not that great, honestly. We're trying to keep our eyes focused on God. He knows our situation and will provide what we need. But it's hard."

"I bet it is." Emma's brain raced, trying to think of something she could do to help. Really help. "I'm honored you're here today when I'm sure you have so many other pressing needs calling you."

"I can only spare the one day, but I didn't want to miss it. It means a lot to my kid brother, and I think this facility will be a real benefit to Jewel Lake. I truly wish you all the best with it."

"Once we're up and running, you and your boys will have to come riding here."

"That would be lovely!" Tammy's face brightened then fell. "Groceries come first, though."

"I wouldn't think of charging you." Emma could hear Vivienne's voice in the back of her head, reminding her they weren't running a charity. But, on the other hand, all the horses would need to be exercised regularly if their owners couldn't make it several times a week. There was a fine line in there somewhere.

"Thanks. That means a lot. We'll have to see how things play out."

"Ready?" Noah's voice interrupted their conversation. "Our group has been assigned to the top of the trail, so let's hike up there and find the flags that define our section. Lead the way, Em."

"Right! Grab your tools, and let's go." She strode toward the back of the corral to the beginning of the trail she, Noah, and Eli had flagged a couple of days back. Her group fell in behind her as the grinding gears of a gravel truck sounded down the drive. Nope. She couldn't be distracted with that. Dealing with the driver was up to Travis and Eli, not her.

"The forest here is great."

Emma blinked to see Josh hiking beside her. "Yeah, I love the smell of the trees. We really tried to save as many as possible, but some of them will have to go."

"We can buck those up for firewood. They should be dry enough to burn by winter."

She grinned. "It's hard to imagine wanting a blaze in my fireplace on such a hot day, but it's Montana. Winter is coming." They'd need to buy their own ATV with a plow on the front to keep the trails cleared then.

"I'm glad we live where there are seasons. This heat makes me appreciate winter more, and the snow makes me appreciate mosquitoes."

"It what?" She laughed.

Josh grinned. "Just checking if you'd tuned me out."

"Ha. Never." Though that might be giving too much away.

The other groups following them had dropped off as they reached their assigned sections, but theirs headed right to the knoll at the top.

"This is where you want to build a gazebo?" Emma's sister-in-law Taryn turned in a circle. "Great view."

"You can see my place from here." Monte pointed to the log ranch house hidden in the distant trees then to the nearer, newer edifice. "Also, Maranatha Inn."

"I love the view," Emma conceded. "I hope no one feels their privacy would be threatened by making this a trail destination?"

Monte shook his head. "I can't see why. If anything, seeing people or horses up here might make folks want to find a way here themselves, maybe by renting a horse from you. My sister and I used to hike up here when we were kids." He indicated the older farmhouse nestled in the Christmas tree farm on this side of the inn. "Although, sometimes, we were just trying to get out of chores."

Emma tried to imagine the gray-headed man as a kid. Failed. He must be even older than Dad.

"Oh, look." Kirk pointed past the tree farm. "There's a bear on the hillside."

Noah pulled out his binoculars and scanned the area. "There must be a berry patch. She's pretty busy in there."

"It won't come over here, will it?" Tammy sounded nervous.

"Not at all likely. Like I said, she's fat and focused."

Emma bit back the comment that there were likely bears much closer than the one they could see. Noah and Monte both had cans of bear spray clipped to their belts in case of a hostile encounter. Bear sightings were common, and it was always good to be prepared. She should carry some herself.

"Okay, the width of the trail is clearly marked." Noah fingered one of the ribbons. "Those of us with chainsaws will cut the trees that are flagged. The logs can be dragged off to the side for now. Any rocks can be shifted to the side as well. Dig up any bushes and toss them aside. Everyone's gonna have sore muscles within an hour, guaranteed."

Emma rotated her shoulders. She was as ready as possible.

Josh flexed his shoulders and tilted his head from side to side. Every muscle in his body burned, including the ones he used daily in handling the forge. Bucking trees and digging out rocks apparently used different muscles... or, at least, in different ways.

"We made decent progress." Emma sounded smugly satisfied.

He glanced at her dirt-and-sweat-smeared face as she dusted her work gloves together. She'd shown up this morning with her long hair braided, wound around her head, and secured under her hat. Now, a twig had caught in one of the escaped tendrils.

Josh reached over and plucked it out of her hair and held it for her inspection.

Her hands flew to her head and her eyes widened. "I bet I'm a mess."

A cute mess. He chuckled and gestured at the dirt staining his Carhartt overalls. "We all are."

Someone from Maranatha Inn had hiked up with sandwiches, fruit, and water at lunchtime. They'd sat on the knoll to rest and admire the view of rolling hills to the west and north. The distant bear seemed to have meandered away. But now, Josh was ready for a hot shower and a thick steak. He was starving.

Should he invite Emma?

No, too soon. Much too soon.

"What are you doing this evening?" he couldn't help asking.

"My parents are cooking dinner for the family. Then their hot tub has my name on it."

"A hot tub sounds great. I'll have to settle for a shower."

"You... never mind."

His heart hiccupped. Had she nearly invited him up to Rockstead? Nah, his overactive imagination had leaped to action. Even he could hardly believe how quickly and thoroughly his emotions had pivoted. It was like someone had cleaned the window glass so he could clearly see what — or who — was on the other side, the woman who'd been obscured by all the smudges of his teen fantasies.

No, he needed to take his time. Twice as much as he probably thought.

"Think we'll be able to get an ATV up here tomorrow to haul some of this out?" Emma looked around at the downed trees strewn in the forest.

Once Noah'd cut a few trees, Josh and Kirk had started trimming branches and cutting the thicker logs into lengths. Everyone had helped stack them along the crude trail.

"Depends on the other crews, honestly. We might need everyone to start at the bottom tomorrow and just keep moving up the trail as it's cleared."

She scrunched her nose to one side. "Yeah, probably. Is it strange I feel ownership of this section our team has been working on?"

Josh chuckled. "It all belongs to you and your sisters."

"Right." She gave her head a shake. "That still seems like crazy talk."

It did. Josh didn't know what to say. His dad and stepmom were still making payments on their own house and were certainly in no position to gift property to him or his sister. Josh could only hope Tammy and Ian would be able to keep up their mortgage payments with Ian off work for so long. Tammy might be serving part-time at the Golden Grill, but he'd bet they were still getting further behind every week.

"Good job, team." Noah high-fived Kirk and then Tammy before sliding his arm around Taryn. "I think we made excellent progress today. If you can make it back tomorrow, great. If not, we understand. I hope everyone has muscle relaxers and a tub with turbo jets! Eight o'clock tomorrow for those who can return."

Tammy linked arms with Emma and Taryn and started down the rough trail as they headed into the section another team had cleared. Okay, then. Josh would stick with the guys. Safer, anyway.

Or so he thought until he heard a blood-curdling scream — then another — from down the trail.

Emma! A bear!

He sprinted around the bend toward the sound of her voice.

Not a bear. A swarm of yellow jackets surrounded her as she stamped her feet, flailed her arms, and screamed some more.

Not the best response. That would only make the stinging insects angrier.

Josh didn't slow down as he scooped Emma into his arms and kept running. He jumped over a log and felt a sting to his neck then another on his arm. He had no hands free to swat, not that it would help.

Rocks and downed trees littered the rough trail. He needed to be careful where he planted his feet. If he twisted his ankle and fell, Emma would be hurt even more than she was now.

Her arms clung to his neck.

He hadn't been stung for at least 30 seconds. Maybe he'd outrun the cloud.

Slow down, Josh. Watch your feet.

But what if she were allergic? What if she were going

into anaphylactic shock? Did he even know what that would look like?

Josh glanced at her face. Her eyes were closed, her long lashes fanned out across her cheeks, but her arms were tight. He'd have to assess when he got to the bottom. He'd find Vivienne first thing. Wasn't she a nurse practitioner? She'd know what to do.

He should take some first aid training.

What if Emma died in his arms?

Most people weren't allergic, but how many stings had she endured? She'd seemed frantic, not a reaction he associated with calm, dependable Emma.

Finally, the stable yard. He scanned the sea of faces and ran straight to Vivienne before skidding to a stop in front of her.

"She's been stung. I don't know how many times."

CHAPTER
Eleven

E mma felt like she'd been attacked by a thousand tiny, poisoned spears.

Oh, wait. She had been... if stingers were spears. And maybe not a thousand? But maybe. There weren't many bits of her body not in intense, throbbing pain.

Thud. Jolt.

Josh had swooped in like an avenging angel and now carried her down the hill over rough terrain at a full run.

It was not comfortable... but still comforting. Of course, he'd do the same for anyone. Maybe he'd even run faster with Alexia.

Emma's twin would never jump off a log straight into a yellow jacket nest. Not that Emma had done it on purpose.

Oh. The. Pain. She tried to swallow the panic. Could she still breathe, or was her throat closing up from an allergic reaction? She'd never reacted before, though. Now, she clung to Josh as he leaped over another obstruction in the debris field that would someday be an actual trail.

Then suddenly he stopped.

She heard the babble of voices.

"Emma? Are you with me?" Vivienne's voice was closest. Clearest.

She opened her eyes and tried to focus on her sister's face. Viv would know what to do. "Yeah," she croaked out.

"How many stings?"

Emma went with her best guess. "A thousand?"

"I bet it feels that way. Here, I'm going to cool you off. Hold your breath for a sec. This will be shocking."

A gallon jug of ice water hit Emma's face, shoulders, and torso. She gasped and stared at her sister. "Was that necessary?" But maybe the pain had slightly reduced.

"I need to get you somewhere where we can assess the stings and get some antihistamines into you. The clinic would be best."

"I'll take her there." Josh.

Viv had probably dumped ice water all over him, too.

"Okay. Why don't I have a full first aid kit here? I should have one. What if I need an epi pen? I'll never be this unprepared again."

"I'm okay, Viv," Emma rasped out. At least, she hoped so.

Her sister snapped her fingers. "To the clinic. Stat."

Josh slid Emma into the passenger seat of his pickup. "We've got this."

Why Josh? Why not Noah? Why didn't Emma just ride with Vivienne? Was all of this really necessary? Maybe. The reprieve of the icy water was already wearing off. Those thousand stings were back with added ferocity.

She was soaked and getting water all over Josh's truck.

A glance across the cab showed water dripping off Josh's set chin. "Thanks."

He shot her a glance and a quick smile as he executed the quickest three-point turn in history. "You're welcome. I hope you'll be okay."

"Me, too." But why wouldn't she be? Everyone got stung once in a while. She'd know by now if she had severe allergies, wouldn't she? But she'd never been stung a thousand times in three seconds before.

It only seemed like another three seconds before Josh squealed to a stop in front of the clinic. Before Emma could do more than unbuckle, he'd opened her door and lifted her out of the cab.

"I can walk."

"I'm carrying you. Where's Vivienne?"

That sounded like honest-to-goodness panic in his voice. Emma put her hand on his cheek to draw his face toward her. "If this were going to kill me, it probably already would have." After all, it must be at least 15 minutes since the attack.

Josh inhaled sharply as his eyes met hers.

She could drown in those dark brown pools, but she forced herself to concentrate. "I won't lie and say I feel great, because I don't, but I don't think I'm going to die."

Brakes squealed, a car door thudded, and pounding footsteps neared. "How is she doing?"

"Okay, I think. She's arguing with me."

"That's Emma for you." Vivienne sounded exasperated.

Why? Emma wasn't trouble. That had always been her twin's position. Sure, Emma had been sucked into it plenty, but she'd rarely been the instigator.

Josh carried her into an exam room and laid her on the table.

"I've got her from here." Vivienne shooed Josh out. "Now, strip, girl. I need to see where all the welts are and assess them. But you can breathe okay?"

"I can breathe."

"Good. I'll grab some antihistamine lotion and ibuprofen. Be right back."

Emma practiced her breathing in a quiet, still environment for a few seconds before removing her T-shirt. Did she really need to strip the rest of the way? There weren't any stings below the belt, were there? Not that she could tell at the moment. All the pulsing bits were higher. And maybe not *quite* a thousand.

Viv bustled back in. She'd thrown a white lab coat over her work clothes and looked every inch a medical professional. Well, unless one saw the dirt-smudged canvas pants below the jacket. She scrubbed in the examination room's sink and turned to Emma. Her eyebrows tilted up. "What part of strip did you not understand?"

"The part where there aren't any stings on my butt or legs. I think my pants and hiking boots kept them out."

"I still want to see for myself, but let's deal with these first." She unscrewed the cap off a lotion bottle and began applying the contents to Emma's welts.

Ten. Eleven. Twelve.

Vivienne stood back and looked Emma over.

"Twelve? Seriously? That's all?"

"It's enough."

She was preaching to the converted. "It felt like way more."

"Drop your pants."

"No, I meant up here." Emma reached to touch her face, but Vivienne's strong fingers grabbed her hand and pushed it down.

"Leave it. Let it do its work. Also, I want to see the rest of you. Oh. Here's ibuprofen. Take it." Viv handed over a paper cup with a couple of pills and another with water.

"Are you always this bossy?" Emma gulped the pills. She could use more water than that, but it was a start.

"You're on my turf, sister dear. I am always this bossy here."

"Good. I guess." Emma stood on unsteady legs and loosened her belt. "I really think this is unnecessary."

Her sister crossed her arms and waited.

Fine. Whatever. Viv better not make any comments about Emma's red lace panties, either.

She didn't. She ran cool eyes over Emma's lower half and nodded. "You're right."

"You think I didn't know where I'd been stung?" Emma pulled her pants back up.

"Good thing you were wearing skinny jeans. Wide pantlegs would have given the yellow jackets easy access upward."

Emma shuddered. She'd be a skinny-jeans girl forever now, no matter what fashion dictated.

"I'll get Eli to take you off of tomorrow's rotation on trail-building so you can rest up."

"I'll decide in the morning. How often do I put on that lotion stuff?" Emma locked eyes with her sister.

Finally, Vivienne rolled her eyes. "You're stubborn."

"Takes one to know one," Emma shot back.

"Twice a day until the swelling subsides. So again tonight and in the morning, and then I'd like to assess again."

Emma held out her hand, and her sister smacked the lotion bottle into her hand. "Thank you."

"And one more thing. You shouldn't be alone tonight."

"I've got the kittens." Which wasn't exactly what Vivienne meant, and she knew it.

"I'll get a foam mattress and sleeping bag and join you."

It would have seemed like a fun slumber party if it weren't for the thousand stings. Okay, only a dozen.

The clinic door burst open, and Emma's family crowded into the tiny waiting room. "How is she?" Alexia demanded.

Josh backed up a step and hit the wall. There was nowhere to go. "Okay, I think. But I haven't heard from her or Vivienne since I left the exam room."

"We'll wait."

Not that there were enough chairs for a quarter of them. All six Cavanagh brothers stood shoulder-to-shoulder in the space, along with their wives and a couple of the older kids. Josh found his boss in the mix and tried to send a telepathic message with his eyes.

"Outside, everyone," Noah ordered. "We can wait under

the tree in the courtyard. Alexia, you wait here with Josh and come right out with word as soon as you hear anything. Got it?"

Alexia saluted.

Travis turned to Nathaniel as they crowded through the door. "I'm gonna run down to the feed store for some insecticidal dust to take out that yellow-jacket nest."

"I'll come with you."

The door closed behind them, and Josh felt like enough air existed to breathe again. Except that Alexia seemed to be inhaling more than her share.

She turned to him. "That was an impressive sprint carrying my sister."

"I wasn't thinking, just acting."

"Looks like you did the right thing."

Josh looked down and poked the tip of his steel-toed boot against a chair leg. "I didn't want her to die."

"Die?"

He heard the incredulity in her voice. "It can happen."

"You were like Superman."

"Not so much." He shook his head and dropped back into the chair he'd been sitting in before the Cavanagh invasion. He rested his elbows on his knees and hung his head. *Lord, please help Emma be okay. Please.*

Even a week ago, he'd have been far more interested in using the moment to pursue Alexia than to worry about Emma. Maybe the switch in his attention was real.

He sensed more than saw Alexia settle into the chair next to him.

"Did anyone else get stung?" she asked.

"I don't even know. She'd gone on ahead with Tammy

and Taryn. I heard her scream." Josh took a ragged breath at the memory. "I ran. Saw her, all frantic, surrounded by insects. Grabbed her and ran all the way down." How far had he run, anyway? A couple of miles? Maybe he *was* Superman. "The trail blurred past. I don't know how I kept from tripping over something. I shouldn't have gone full tilt like that. I could have dropped her and broken her neck."

"You didn't. That's the main thing." Alexia's boot nudged his. "All while wearing heavy footwear, no less."

Was that admiration he heard? Or maybe his old infatuation tried to hear encouragement where there never had been any.

He shifted in his chair, putting his feet further from hers. "Anyone would have done it."

"No one else did. Not even her big brother."

Also true, but it didn't mean anything. He hadn't made a conscious decision to sweep in and save the day.

"I just want to say thanks. People think I'm an airhead, but I'm not. I care about my sisters." Alexia rested her hand on his arm. "I don't know what I'd do if anything happened to either one of them. Em, especially. We shared a womb, after all. She's been part of me my entire life."

A rustle behind the desk alerted him, and he looked up to see Emma and Vivienne standing there. Emma's gaze flitted from her twin to him, resting for a second on Alexia's hand on his arm.

Josh surged to his feet, as did Alexia beside him, dropping the contact. "Are you okay?"

Emma gave a cautious smile. "I think so. Viv fixed me up. Thanks for acting so quickly."

"My pleasure."

Alexia scoffed. "Right, like you always wanted to run a couple of miles down a hill carrying a woman."

"Don't forget wearing work boots." But his eyes were focused on Emma. She had several pale smears on her face and throat. Coating the stings?

"I can't thank you enough, either," Vivienne said. "You guys should clear out of here now, though. I'll clean up the exam room and be over to Happy Trails in about an hour and a half. Can someone stay with her until I get there with my camping gear?"

"I can." Josh's words were quick and automatic.

Alexia elbowed him. "I've got it. No need to go out of your way. If there's a sister sleepover happening, I'm all in."

Josh quelled a rush of impatience. Whose side was she on, anyway? First, she urged him to pursue Emma, then she got in his way. Not that he'd be invited to any sleepover. Uh... not that he wanted to be.

"You need to get your stuff, too. Why don't you bring a pizza when you come? I'll leave her to you two then."

"I vote for takeout from the Golden Grill." Emma turned to Alexia. "I'm starving. You know what I like."

Alexia shrugged and studied Josh for a few seconds. "Okay. Your wish is my command. Oh! Our brothers are outside waiting for news." She charged out the door like the whirlwind she was.

Vivienne's footsteps disappeared down the short corridor.

Josh turned to Emma. "Ready? You look a whole lot better than you did half an hour ago." Less on death's door.

113

"I guess that's a compliment?" Emma's eyebrows arched.

"It is. It really is." He held out his elbow, but she didn't take it.

Was she truly prepared for the onslaught of all her brothers just outside the door? Josh didn't think he was.

CHAPTER
Twelve

"How are you feeling now?"

That must have been the tenth repeat of Josh's question in as many minutes as they drove toward Happy Trails. Emma stifled a surge of impatience. "I'm fine."

Each of her sisters-in-law had given her a hug and examined her visible welts and said how grateful they were to Josh for acting so quickly. Yeah, yeah, so was she. She hadn't been about to die, regardless of what everyone seemed to think.

Had she been very unpleasantly uncomfortable? Absolutely, yes. She'd panicked. She knew better than to flail around — it only made the yellow jackets angrier, and each had the capacity to sting multiple times, unlike honeybees.

Josh had hoisted her into his arms and run without asking if she needed help. He'd simply assumed. She'd hung on for dear life because all she could envision was him tripping over an exposed root and falling. Now *that* would have been life threatening.

And yes, some people were allergic to insect venom. Not her, or she'd have figured it out much younger, with how often she'd been stung as a kid.

But Josh didn't know that. He'd acted like a caveman.

A caveman.

For her.

Everyone acted like he'd saved her life. It had almost seemed romantic until she'd come out of the examination room and seen Alexia's hand on Josh's arm as she gazed adoringly up at him.

He'd finally gotten his wish. Alexia had noticed him. Booyah for them both, and now Josh was stuck hauling Emma's carcass home instead of hanging out with Alexia.

"I was so worried about you."

She forced down her irritation. "I guess one good thing came out of all the excitement."

Josh glanced her way, eyebrows up. "Oh?"

"You got your wish with Alexia. She seems to have overcome her aversion to you." Man, she should watch her tongue. Maybe the insects' venom had gotten more than skin deep. "Sorry you're stuck taking me home."

"Emma."

She deserved the forcefulness in his voice. "Sorry I'm so much trouble."

"*Emma.*"

"What?" She resisted the urge to touch the burning welts. Experience had taught her they'd only hurt worse if she gave in. Somehow, she couldn't resist the same thing with Josh, even knowing the pain.

"I didn't rescue you for Alexia's sake."

"Right. Because I was such a dolt up there. I—"

"Would you listen to me?" He flicked on the turn signal beside the Happy Trails sign. "I care about *you*, Emma."

"You... what?" Obviously, the fiery itch twisted his words in her mind.

"Is that so hard to believe?"

"You were chasing my sister hard for ages. And now in the blink of an eye, you change? Right. Tell that to someone more gullible than me. I'm not buying it." She turned her face toward the window so he wouldn't be able to see the tears forming in her eyes. Stupid pain. She could blame her reaction on that, right? On all the trauma of the past hour or two?

"I'm sorry I hurt you that way."

In what way? But she wouldn't ask. She needed some distance from this man and the entire day's emotional overload. After the pain meds kicked in, she'd be able to file everything in tidy little boxes and be in control again. Right now, the soothing cream Vivienne had applied seemed to be losing the battle against the burn.

Josh parked in front of her house. Her brothers had argued she should come up to Rockstead for the night, but she'd insisted on coming home to the kittens. Her sisters would be enough, especially with Vivienne's medical expertise. She didn't need her parents and all her brothers and their wives hovering over her, too. The hot tub wouldn't feel as good as she'd anticipated.

Emma turned to Josh. "Thanks for the ride. Sorry I've been such lousy company. I think I'll have a nap until my sisters come, so you don't need to bother coming in."

"I'm coming in." He jumped out of the driver's door and, before she could register his intention, he jogged around the front, opened the passenger door, and reached for her.

She smacked his hand away. "I'm capable of walking, thank you very much."

Josh took a step back and gestured for her to prove it.

Fine. She would. She slid out of the high cab. His truck seriously needed running boards. Just because he was tall… no, no more thoughts about how he was no longer the scrawny kid from high school.

Emma marched up the front walk — or where it would be one day soon — and opened the door. The aroma of hardwood floors, wood sealer, and dust invaded her nostrils just as the kittens scampered into the foyer, meowing like they hadn't seen a human for days if not weeks.

"Wow, they've grown." Josh bent and scooped up the orange tabby. "Blaze, right?"

She blinked. He remembered? "Yes. The calico is Tangle, and the tortie is Coonie. And, apparently, they are starving to the death."

"Let me."

"Josh. Seriously. I'm not an invalid." She grabbed a scoop of kitten kibble from the bag in the closet and dumped it in their bowl. Then she pressed the battery-operated pump on the five-gallon water jug on her camping table to top up their water bowl. "That will keep them busy for a bit."

Too bad she couldn't think of anything to keep Josh busy, though he was looking around. He'd spotted… oh, no.

"The flowers really brighten up the space, don't they?"

Emma inhaled. Exhaled. How had she never wondered if he'd come in and see them still in her possession? "Alexia's place is in the midst of drywalling, so it's too dusty for them to survive over there."

Josh grimaced. "I'm sorry I put you in the middle of that. That was stupid of me. Immature."

He wasn't wrong, but still. "She might want them now."

"Emma." Josh turned toward her. He stood nearby.

Too near. She backed up a step. "It's fine, Josh. You don't need to pretend."

"I'm not pretending. I've been feeling differently toward you for a while now."

It hadn't been that long since he'd dropped off the flowers. A week? Two? She'd had to pluck out dead blossoms already. On closer inspection, she should just ditch the things. They looked their age, and they didn't belong to her. She could stick the empty vase in Alexia's place for her to deal with however she wanted.

"Emma."

He kept saying her name, but he didn't need to fake interest. She turned, sweeping her hand. "Do you like the color palette? I love green, and the warm tones of the alder flooring go so well with it, I think. There are different shades of green in the various rooms. Down that little hallway are the two spare bedrooms. I mean, they'll likely be kids' bedrooms one day. Oh, who am I kidding? I'll probably never have any. But Alexia's place has five bedrooms, and she doesn't even want kids at all. Not that it matters. I mean, it might matter to you, so maybe that's why I'm telling you. Me, on the other hand, I like children. That's why I'm a teacher. But Alexia—"

Josh's mouth covered hers.

For one brief instant, she melted into his embrace. His kiss. It felt like coming home. Then reality hit, and she surged backward out of his arms. "Why did you do that? To shut me up? I was babbling, right? It's the pain meds. You should go. You really should. My sisters will be here any minute now."

"It wasn't to shut you up." A flicker of amusement caught in his eyes. "Well, maybe a little. But I kissed you because I wanted to kiss *you*."

Emma didn't miss the emphasis, but she chalked it up to hallucinations from the ibuprofen. She could blame a lot on that. Anything and everything, really. "You're supposed to ask the girl's permission."

"May I kiss you again?"

"You absolutely may not." If only she could have put more confidence into that refusal. Those few seconds had been the most amazing of her entire life, but no matter what he said, it had been a mistake. He'd forgotten for a minute that she wasn't Alexia. Not that they looked that much alike.

Great. Her brain was still misfiring in every conceivable direction. She pointed to the door. "Please leave now."

Josh shook his head slowly, his gaze never leaving hers. "I promised your medical provider I'd stay with you until she came."

"Outside on the step."

"Only if you are there, too."

Emma wanted a nap in the worst way. Her stomach growled. Okay, maybe she had two things on the brain. Three, if she counted kissing Josh.

Nope. Not counting that.

"You're living here now?"

"I'm sort of camping. I have a Coleman stove out on the deck. The crew is nearly done with the hardwood, then the tile floors and plumbing fixtures are next."

"It looks really nice. Mind if I look around?"

"Go for it." She picked up Tangle and dropped into her foldable deck chair to pet the kitten. Immediately, a rumbling purr greeted her ears.

Emma watched Josh poke into the two bedrooms and bathroom on the one side of the great room then cross the alder floor to peek into the master. It didn't escape her notice that he didn't go all the way in. What was he thinking? Not that it mattered. Her choices didn't affect him in any way. She didn't care whether he liked her house or not.

He'd kissed her.

But it hadn't meant anything. She'd been blabbing on and on *and on.*

It had felt really, really nice. It had awakened something inside her, something that had lain dormant since they were both 16 and in English Lit class together. They'd been dissecting Charles Dickens' writing style, and Emma had eagerly cited it as lively and humorous with injections of profound depth. Josh had countered that the same could be said of a Louis L'Amour novel. Emma had gone home and borrowed *Bendigo* from her father's bookcase... and she'd had to agree with Josh. She'd never told him that. She wasn't going there today, either.

Josh lowered himself to the floor and leaned against the wall beside her bedroom doorway after testing to make sure the paint had dried. Blaze jumped on his knee and demanded petting, while Coonie sat back, watching. "What kind of cabinetry are you going with?"

Emma blinked. She'd expected... what? "Red alder like the floors. The floors in both bathrooms, the kitchen, and the mudroom-slash-laundry-room will be tiled, so wood will look great on the cabinets and tie everything together."

"Sounds nice." His gaze bounced off hers before he focused on the cat in his lap. "You've done great."

"It's all been Brent and his crew."

"You picked everything. You did the painting. Probably other things."

"Okay. You're right. I did a good job." So long as one didn't look too closely at some of the paint edges. Cutting in was harder than it looked.

"I shouldn't have kissed you. I'm sorry, but not sorry."

So was she. Sorry but not sorry, that is. "Apology accepted." There was that prim teacher voice again. Why couldn't she just be herself?

Because Josh didn't truly want her. He was either looking for Alexia or an Alexia stand-in. He didn't see Emma as a desirable woman on her own. Emma had felt second-best at everything all her life. Everything except school, that is, so she'd pushed herself to excel in the one arena where her twin couldn't best her.

Outgoing Alexia. Fun-loving Alexia. Fearless Alexia. She rode Destiny bareback like the wind.

Emma was more cautious. Held back more, which seemed to be both her weakness and her strength. Today, she'd cling to it as an advantage. She was not going to throw herself at Josh and pretend he'd meant that kiss as anything to remember.

But she'd never forget it, brief as it had been.

At least half an hour remained before one or both of her sisters would rescue her, and Josh seemed determined to stay right here until officially relieved of duty.

Duty, that's all it was. Somehow, he felt responsible. Silly, of course.

"Tell me what you've been up to since high school. How did you decide to become a farrier? When did you start as Noah's apprentice? That all happened when I was away at college."

Josh raised his eyebrows and looked directly at her.

Busted. He could tell what she was doing. She didn't want to talk about kissing, and he knew it. He should be relieved that she was changing the subject, because he likely didn't want to further discuss it, either. Except he'd brought it up twice.

Never mind. Not going there.

Emma smiled at Josh. "Please tell me?"

CHAPTER
Thirteen

J osh let himself into his sister's house. "Tammy?"

She appeared in the living room doorway. "Hey, Josh. The boys are in bed."

Made sense. It was 7:30. Alexia had invited him to stay at Happy Trails for takeout. She'd even picked up a burger for him, assuming he'd accept her invitation, so he had. He was a bachelor who didn't love cooking for just himself. Of course, he'd stayed.

He poked at the floor with his work boot and glanced at his sister. "I kissed her."

"Alexia? *Josh!*"

"No. Emma."

Tammy blinked and gave her head a shake. "Why don't you come in and tell Ian and me all about it?"

A guy wasn't supposed to kiss and tell, but this wasn't locker-room bragging rights happening here. He needed someone to help him sort out his confusion. Dad had always told Josh that guys didn't have feelings. Real men acted on evidence, not emotions.

Maybe that's why Dad had been married three times.

"Honey, my brother is here to download his romantic problems for our consideration." Tammy nestled in next to Ian on the sofa and smirked at Josh expectantly.

Why had he come here again? Because none of his old buddies lived in town anymore. Tammy and Ian were the closest friends he had to bounce things off of.

Ian shifted, grimacing, then clasped Tammy's hand. "Bring it."

"I had a crush on Alexia Cavanagh forever."

Tammy swept her free hand. "Old news. Get to the new part." She leaned into Ian and whispered loudly, "He kissed Emma."

Josh closed his eyes for a second and kept his growl inside. Maybe he should have relied on only God for his tell-all.

"By mistake?" Ian sounded incredulous.

Josh shook his head and met his brother-in-law's gaze. "On purpose."

"Oh, boy."

"Yeah. Listen, how did you know Tammy was the right woman for you? I mean, she can be pretty annoying."

Ian smirked. "You've noticed that, too?"

Tammy smacked Ian's arm, and he laughed.

That. Josh wanted to get there with Emma. He blinked. He did? The idea had certainly grown on him. She fit with him so much better than her twin did.

"So… me and Tammy." Ian rubbed the stubble on his jaw. "I have to say, I was oblivious at first. I played sports. No time for girls."

"I chased him down." Tammy bobbed her eyebrows at Josh.

"That's the truth of it." Ian leaned over and kissed her temple. "You know your sister. When she makes up her mind about something, a guy might as well fall in line from the start. It's gonna happen, and you have two choices. You can climb onboard or get run over."

"The thing is, Emma doesn't believe that I'm over her sister."

"Didn't you buy Alexia flowers like a week ago?" Tammy gave him a pointed look.

"Two." But, yeah, recently.

"Patience, bucko." Ian leaned back against the sofa pillow. "You're 25. Not exactly dying of old age any minute soon. You can take your time."

"You're a lofty 28. You were married and a father when you were my age."

"And we're not the same guy. Some of us mature more quickly than others." Ian smirked.

"Gee, thanks for calling me an immature kid."

Tammy chuckled. "A guy who kisses a girl a week — excuse me, two weeks — after giving her sister flowers? If the shoe fits, wear it. Also, how is Emma doing? You texted that she was okay, but is she, really?"

Josh shrugged one shoulder. "I think so." Possibly high on pain meds, but that was a different tale. "Vivienne is staying with her tonight to make sure, but the welts are already subsiding."

"That was an impressive run." Tammy turned to Ian. "You should have seen him. He picked her up and sprinted down the entire mountain carrying her like it was an Olympic event."

In the caveman era, it might have been. Josh flushed. "I was afraid. You remember Starla."

"I know." Tammy's voice softened. "I've told you about her, right, Ian? Starla was our dog when we were kids. It's rare that a dog dies of anaphylactic shock, but she did."

"I'm sorry, love." Ian stroked Tammy's hand. "I don't fault you for reacting like that, Josh. I'd have done the same for Tammy. Or maybe anyone, if I didn't have a busted kneecap."

"Is it healing better now?" Josh eyed Tammy, since Ian couldn't be trusted to tell the truth on this topic, and Tammy was usually at work when Josh came to watch the boys.

"Sure."

But Tammy rocked her hand back and forth slightly.

"How much longer in the cast, do you think?"

"A few more weeks." Ian grimaced.

That long? Weren't broken bones supposed to heal in six to eight weeks? Maybe busted kneecaps took longer. Maybe recovering from major surgery requiring a rod and multiple screws took longer.

"Next comes physical therapy. Forgive me for not looking forward to more pain."

"It sounds rough, man."

"You have no idea. It's made only marginally more bearable by having a wife to wait on me hand and foot. Except she abandoned me today."

"Hey, you said I should help at Happy Trails, and Grandma had the boys."

"I know. Still had to fend for myself." Ian sounded morose, but he winked at Josh where Tammy couldn't see.

"How did it go with Grandma?"

"She said they were fine, but she looked exhausted, and she didn't invite them back."

"Didn't she tell you she was used to wrangling two males?" Josh couldn't help but laugh.

"I'm pretty sure managing the church office for Pastor Marshall and Pastor Eli isn't the same thing as two preschoolers." Tammy shook her head. "I don't know how much longer she'll be working there, though. Remember her heart attack?"

"Yeah?" How could Josh ever forget the trauma of that day several years ago? They'd all congregated in the hospital waiting room with little guarantee she'd survive, but she'd been too stubborn to die.

"I think her heart is acting up again. Isn't it time she retired and took up crocheting or something?"

Ian chuckled. "She lives for that place."

"But her life would be so much more peaceful," Tammy countered.

"She doesn't want peace. She thrives on knowing what everyone in town is up to. Or at least everyone in the church. Where will she get her intel if she isn't in the thick of it?"

"I'm with Ian," Josh put in. "I can't see her retiring. At least, not until Pastor Marshall does. Isn't he in his sixties now? That day has to be coming."

"Then she'll want to whip the new pastor into shape." Ian held up both hands. "I didn't mean that literally. But she lives to know."

"You're not wrong," Josh agreed. "Grandpa is a saint to put up with her."

"And I'm a saint to put up with your sister."

"Hey!" Tammy swatted Ian's arm. "What about me being the best thing that ever happened to you?"

"Oh, yeah. I forgot for a minute." He nuzzled her hair.

Josh knew when he was being dismissed. Did he have an answer to his problem? Not exactly or, at least, not one he liked.

He was not particularly fond of patience.

Emma awoke to gentle snoring. Vivienne? What was she doing here... right. The stings. Emma assessed herself. One part itchy. Nine parts hungry. And Brent's crew would be coming today to start installing tile floors. The sooner the better. She might have a working toilet by the weekend.

She rolled off the camp cot and tiptoed out into the great room, where sunshine streamed in through the windows on either side of the as-yet-unfinished fireplace. She'd loved that look in the Sweet River Ranch lodge's great room so much it had undoubtedly played into her choice of floor plans here. She stretched, slid her feet into flip flops, and headed out to the biffy at the corner of Sisters Close. Back to wash her hands in a basin — a sink would be almost as welcome as a toilet — and then she prepped her coffeepot and flipped it on.

It stood at the other end of the folding table from Josh's

flowers. She plucked out a couple of dead blossoms and a few droopy leaves. She should pitch the whole bouquet today. Its beauty had been spent. Keeping it only made people ask stupid questions.

Josh had noticed.

Josh had kissed her.

Because she'd been babbling. Oh, he'd said that wasn't why, but of course, he was just being nice about it. She'd certainly been prattling on and on. No wonder he'd wanted silence, if only for a few seconds.

Why couldn't it have been real? Yeah, he'd asked to kiss her again, but that was to save face. He knew she'd say no. Because why would she say yes? That would only have revealed her pathetic crush.

No, Josh wasn't the guy for her, no matter how heroic he'd been getting her to medical help yesterday. Unnecessarily heroic.

"Hey." Alexia stumbled out of the bedroom, rubbing her eyes. "Do I smell coffee?"

"Of course, you do. I've been up for ten minutes."

"Need some."

"Wait until it beeps."

Alexia grimaced. "I have to pee, anyway."

"Outside."

"I don't know how you can stand living here in this mess. The kittens would have been fine at the ranch. Noah even said he'd take them in, and we could have gotten cats later when we were ready for them."

"I couldn't stand *not* living here, no matter how inconvenient."

"I don't think you could possibly have said what I

thought I heard." Alexia stomped into her cowboy boots —
which looked a tiny bit ridiculous with her pink baby-doll
pajamas — and hiked out the door.

Blaze stretched his way out of the basket under the
table, and Emma picked him up to nuzzle him. Last night,
he'd been Josh's kitten. He'd crawled right into the guy's
lap and had a nap. Cats could do anything without being
judged for their motives.

"I know Noah used to take us camping when we were
kids." Alexia had returned. "But then we slept in a tent in
the woods to get away from Dad and his temper."

Also, away from Mom and her depression. Emma
raised her eyebrows. "Your point is?"

"Dad's not so bad anymore."

"I'm not running *away*, Lex. I'm running *to*. It's a big
difference. This is our future."

"Yeah, well, my future has running water in it." Grimacing, Alexia scrubbed in the basin of lukewarm water. "Will
I need my travel mug from the truck?"

"Of course, you will. I'm not set up for company."

Alexia glared and headed back out the door just as Vivienne came from the bedroom, already dressed and looking
put together. "Good morning."

"Hey, Viv. How did you sleep?"

"The floor is hard."

Emma hadn't invited her sisters to a sleepover.

"How is your face?" Vivienne leaned in, examining the
welts. "Good. The reaction is down considerably. Do you
want me to apply the lotion this morning, or do you want to?"

"I'll do it."

"I'm so glad you're feeling better." Vivienne hugged her. "You had me worried there yesterday."

"Because Josh overreacted and made everyone else do the same."

"He cares about you."

Emma huffed a laugh. "Sure. That's what happened. Hey, if you have a travel mug in your car, you can have some coffee. I made a full pot."

Viv wrinkled her nose. "Tea?"

"Sorry, I don't have any."

"You're seriously roughing it."

"I don't drink tea, in case you've forgotten." The coffee maker burbled to a stop and beeped. "Coffee, on the other hand, is life."

"I thought that was Jesus."

"Him, too."

Alexia's hand blocked hers when Emma reached for the coffee pot. "'Scuse me."

"Look, if you're okay, I think I'll head into town, get cleaned up at the apartment, and make myself some tea."

Alexia stirred a heaping spoonful of sugar into her coffee. "It's a trail workday again."

Vivienne sighed. "I'll be back."

"Pinky promise?"

"What, are we in grade school? I'll be back... bringing breakfast for all of us."

"Sounds fair. I doubt Emma has enough on hand to feed us."

"Truth." Emma doctored her coffee and took a sip. "Ah. The day looks better already. I'll get dressed and have my

Bible reading while you're gone, then I'll be ready for another day on the trail."

Her hand on the knob, Vivienne frowned. "You should take it easy today."

"Why? I'm fine. Really."

"It's your funeral." Vivienne swept out.

"She needs caffeine," Alexia observed.

"Don't we all? Caffeine and Jesus."

"Right. Of course. I'm taking my cup out to your deck. That's a great view you've got."

"That's why I picked this lot." No need to remind Alexia she hadn't seemed to care about any of the details at the beginning. Or even a few weeks ago.

"You'd better do a good job of covering up those red marks or Joshy won't believe you're fine. You look terrible."

"You're so good for a girl's ego. And why would I care what Josh thinks?"

"Right." Alexia smirked and let herself out the French doors.

How awkward was it going to be around Josh today after everything that had happened yesterday?

That kiss!

CHAPTER

Fourteen

I t was the evening of the third trail-building day. Josh had managed to keep from hovering over Emma, but it had taken all his self-control. The swelling around the stings appeared down considerably, though, and she insisted she was okay.

Fewer folks had shown up on the second day, which had worked out fine. They'd put several ATVs and trailers into action, hauling branches and bushes down and heaping them into a big pile in the middle of the Happy Trails parking area, far from any other combustibles.

Today, they'd finished clearing the brush and dragging out logs while the Cavanagh brothers hauled gravel up. Travis packed the new trail with the roller on his skid-steer.

Josh tossed a match into the pile of branches as everyone gathered around. He'd be on his best behavior tonight. Declan and Kathryn were present for the bonfire and the picnic that marked the finale of this project.

What must it have been like to grow up in such a

large family? Yeah, Josh remembered from high school that it hadn't all been sunshine and roses for them. The parents had split up for a year or two back then. That had put the twins into Creekside Academy for high school. He'd seen them at church and youth group before that, but it was in class that he'd really gotten to know them... and become obsessed with the wrong sister.

He grimaced at the memory of how blatant he'd been in his pursuit. He'd even talked to Pastor Eli about how to get Alexia's attention. Pastor Eli and Harper were here tonight, too.

"Hey, there, son."

Josh blinked and turned to the voice. He surged to his feet. "Mr. Cavanagh. Good to see you, sir."

"Declan."

Yeah, right. The man might have tamed his temper over the years, but he was still intimidating. He was not only the father of Josh's boss, but of the girl he hoped to win. Did Josh really want to be part of this huge, testosterone-laden clan?

"This has been quite the project. You were here every day?"

"Yes, sir. I know they'll need more trails than this one, but it's a good start."

Declan nodded thoughtfully as he looked around the place. "The stable looks solid. The girls' houses are coming along well. Emma's even living here already." The man chuckled. "Says she likes camping out. Who knew?"

Josh smiled but said nothing.

"Anyway, I think we can start putting out word that

Happy Trails is ready to take on boarders. Have you bought yourself a horse yet to keep here?"

"Me?" Josh couldn't keep the incredulity out of his voice. "No." He hadn't taken time to look into it.

Declan frowned. "This is a great opportunity for you. A farrier should have his own mount. It will help you become more comfortable with horses."

"I can't deny that, sir." Noah paid him decently, but a horse cost a lot to buy and maintain… even with the ability to keep it shod on his own.

"Kathryn has picked up a new mare for herself, and no one is really riding Laire these days. You'd be doing me a favor giving her a home down here and riding her once or twice a week. She's a good mare, just not up to the long rides in the high country that we like to do."

"Sir?" Josh blinked. "You're giving me a horse?"

Declan shrugged. "Call it a loan, if you prefer. If Laire needs veterinary attention, give me a call, and I'll take care of it."

"I don't know what to say."

"How about yes?"

"Uh, sure. Yes. Thank you."

"We have a special saddle for her I'll bring along when I transport her. She has a bit of a sway back."

Josh nodded dumbly. "Okay."

Declan clapped Josh on the shoulder. "Good. I'm glad we have that taken care of. I'll talk to the girls about when I can bring her down, along with a couple of other older horses they will use for kiddy lessons. That will leave them boarding space for another twelve. Do you know if any of those box stalls are spoken for already?"

"I couldn't tell you. I've been focused on the smithy and, the past few days, on the trail."

"Right." Declan looked out over the crowd.

Someone had set a cooler full of hot dogs and a huge box of buns on a long table. Condiments, bags of chips, and a couple of grocery-store veggie platters and fruit trays covered the remainder of the space. Partway around the bonfire, Caleb Grant sat in a foldable chair and strummed his guitar with kids gathered around.

This celebration had gotten much larger than Josh had anticipated. He'd thought they'd torch the branches, wait until the flames died out, and call it a day. He should have known the Cavanaghs would make a party out of it, though.

Declan took Josh's arm and steered him the other direction. Too late, Josh realized where they were headed.

"Girls!" Declan called.

All three turned to their father... and Josh.

"I was just telling Josh here that I'll bring Laire down for him to ride. You've also got two other horses pegged for beginners. What day do you want the horses delivered? Because I think you're about ready to open for business."

"You're giving Mom's mare to Josh?" Alexia's eyebrows rose.

"Loaning." Declan let go of Josh. "Can't be a man who works with horses without having easy access to one of his own."

Josh straightened, feeling his chest puff out a little at being declared a man. But what did it matter what Declan thought of him? Oh, a lot.

Emma shook her head. "We don't even have all the

plumbing in yet, Dad. We're hand-pumping water for the horses already here."

"I thought Callahan was putting power to that pump. What's the holdup? Is he here somewhere?" Declan frowned and looked around.

"No, this party is for the trail crew. Nothing to do with the timber-framers."

"Huh. Well, I guess I'll drive down tomorrow and talk to the man. We need to get things stepped up around here. Priorities and all." He focused on Emma. "You don't have running water at the house yet, either?"

"Coming soon, Dad. While we've been building trails, the tilers have been working on the floors. Grout is going in tomorrow, so toilets and showers are expected Monday. The sinks will take longer because the cabinetry isn't ready yet."

"Vivienne? Alexia? Status report?"

Part of Josh wanted to slink away, but the part that wanted in on this family bolted his boots to the ground.

The sisters exchanged glances. "Mine is about two weeks behind Emma's," Vivienne said at last. "Alexia's is about that far behind mine."

A peek at the man beside him revealed a pulsing jugular. "An entire month or more? What am I paying that man for?"

Alexia linked her arm to her dad's. "It's on me, Dad. Don't blame Brent. He's had to reschedule some subcontractors."

Josh blinked. Alexia was actually taking responsibility for her own indecision?

Then he saw a van pulling into the yard, and his eyes grew wide.

Emma shouldn't have been watching Josh, but she couldn't help herself. The main thing was that he hadn't seemed to catch her peeking at him. Not yet, anyway. But when his attention was caught by something beyond her, she turned to see.

Tammy hopped out of the van's driver's door and scurried around the front to open the other side. A moment later, Ian appeared on crutches. Two little boys blasted past their parents... and collided with Josh.

"Hey, slow down. That bonfire is really, really hot and can hurt you." He lifted the littlest one into his arms while the bigger one clung to his leg.

Josh looked good with kids, a thought Emma should not be having. *He kissed me!* But it hadn't meant anything beyond stopping her from prattling nonsense as the shock wore off.

Yeah, she needed to stop thinking about that kiss. It hadn't even been a good one, barely a connection before she'd jerked away. She'd had much sweeter kisses from some of the guys she'd dated in college, but none had been as electrifying as that awkward instant with Josh's lips on hers.

And why was she standing in the middle of a crowd of 40 people gathered around a huge bonfire thinking about something that had happened two days ago? She'd managed to avoid him ever since, even though they'd worked the same trail-building crew. She'd keep avoiding him until she could meet his gaze without heat rushing up her neck. It could take a while. Maybe until she turned 50.

But now Tammy studied her face. "You look so much better, Emma!"

"Um, thanks?"

The other woman chuckled. "You always look great. You know what I mean."

"I do. Thanks for your help the other day." Emma smiled at Ian. "And thank you for sparing your wife."

"It meant a lot to her." The man shifted on his crutches, his casted leg sticking out in front. "She wanted to come tonight, too, but there's a lot of people."

"I'll get your lawn chair. Then people are less likely to run into your leg." Tammy turned and jogged away.

"Thanks, love." Ian studied Emma. "You're building a great thing here."

And where were her sisters? Because surely Ian meant all three of them, but Vivienne and Alexia had drifted away with their heads together. Dad, too, stood around the other side of the bonfire.

Now she smiled at Ian. "Thanks. Someday you can come riding here." Didn't look to be imminent with the way he carried that leg.

A little hand tugged on her own, and she looked down to see Soren peering up at her. "Do you ride a horse?"

She grinned at the awe in the little boy's voice as she squatted to his level. "I do ride a horse. Her name is Desiree."

"Is she big? Does she buck you off?"

"She's pretty big and, no, she doesn't buck." She'd been feisty as a filly, but Nathaniel had worked with her until she'd settled down. Nat had all the patience in the world.

"I wants ta ride a horse."

"You'll get a chance, I promise."

"Don't make promises you can't keep," Ian warned.

Emma looked up. "I'm pretty sure I can keep this one, unless you tell me you don't want your kids anywhere near horses."

"Can't afford it."

"I'm not asking for money. You guys are my friends."

Tammy arrived and set up the chair, and Ian lowered himself into it, closing his eyes against what looked like pain by the grimace. "Of course, we're friends!" Tammy looked between them. "What are we talking about?"

"Miss Emma says I can ride a horse, Mommy!"

"Oh!" Tammy's gaze met Emma's.

"You don't even need Miss Emma for that," Josh interjected. "Mr. Cavanagh offered me one of his wife's older horses for me to ride. I can take Soren and even Blaine sometime."

Emma looked up at Josh from where she knelt on the ground. "I'm amazed my dad made that offer. He doesn't trust just anyone."

Josh's eyes warmed as he shifted Blaine to his other arm. "What can I say? I was surprised, too."

"Well, look at you, little brother." Tammy reached for Blaine, who twisted away and clung to Josh's neck. "Getting all cozy with your boss's family."

"Not on purpose."

It was too dark to tell for sure, but Emma would lay good money on Josh's face reddening with embarrassment. He met her eyes about as briefly as his mouth had two days ago before he averted his gaze.

Was there any chance he'd actually meant that kiss? He'd seemed to be trying to tell her that he saw *her*, Emma, not her twin. But it had been only 24 hours since she'd pitched out the bouquet he'd given Alexia. What guy could do an about-face that quickly?

Soren turned from Emma and reached for his uncle. Somehow Josh lifted him while not relinquishing his hold on the younger brother.

Emma rose from her crouched position, unable to look away from Josh interacting with his two nephews. He seemed to have a great relationship with the boys. Kids were good judges of character, right? That meant he had to be a decent guy.

She already knew that. He'd been fixated on Alexia since Emma could remember, but after the day he'd dropped off the flowers, all evidence pointed to him having abandoned that pursuit.

He'd said he saw *her*, Emma.

Was she easier to catch, like some kind of consolation prize? She hardened her heart, but her defenses needed constant shoring up like a rickety pier in the face of a hurricane.

Especially if he kept looking at her the way he did right now, between the demands of two little boys.

Because that softness in his eyes? It was directed straight at Emma.

CHAPTER

Fifteen

E mma slipped into her family's pew at Creekside
Fellowship on Sunday morning with seconds to
spare before the worship leader stepped up to the
mic. Alexia tapped her sports watch and glared at Emma.

Hey, she'd made it on time. The plumbers had finished
the basic restroom over in the stable. It held only a toilet,
sink, and prefab shower stall on a polished concrete floor,
but after the past few weeks, it was pure luxury. Emma
might have gotten a little carried away standing under a
hot waterfall this morning, but she was here now, and her
twin could chill out.

"Be bold! Be strong!" Caleb's voice rang out from the
platform as the drummer set the tempo.

Emma loved this song, even though she was a chicken
at heart. Or maybe *because* she was a chicken. The next few
songs were also about courage. Emma sensed a theme long
before Pastor Marshall took the pulpit and read from the
first chapter of Joshua. "This is my command — be strong

and courageous! Do not be afraid or discouraged. For the Lord your God is with you wherever you go."

She'd claimed this verse long ago when she'd headed away from home to college. Yes, she'd still had her twin with her, but everything had been so different from the ranch. Even though the house where she'd grown up had burned to the ground during her teen years, Rockstead had always lived up to its name: steady as a rock, a firm foundation beneath her feet.

But her true rock was Jesus. She'd memorized the first few verses of Psalm 18 back then: *I love you, Lord; you are my strength. The Lord is my rock, my fortress, and my savior; my God is my rock, in whom I find protection. He is my shield, the power that saves me, and my place of safety.*

Emma settled into the pew and listened to Pastor Marshall expound on the theme of biblical courage, not a matter of ego or determination, but utter confidence in the power of a loving God.

Why couldn't she stop being so afraid? How could she shy away when God commanded her to be brave? She didn't need to be abrasive or confrontational. Quietly strong was okay, but what would that even look like?

Pastor Marshall paused for a moment, leaning on the pulpit. His face seemed a little off color, almost gray. But before Emma could panic, he resumed his sermon. Maybe he cut it a little short, but it had done its work in Emma's heart. She had something to think about.

Caleb led the closing hymn, "Be Still My Soul," and Emma felt her soul doing just that, quieting itself before her Maker. She'd been fretting and feeling responsible for her sisters, she'd been hovering over all the construction at Happy Trails, she'd been working on English Lit lesson plans until the wee hours, and she'd even been worried about the kittens. She'd taken too much on herself and forgotten that not everything on the planet required her personal attention.

Some of it did, like the upcoming school year.

But even there, she could rest on God. Such a difficult concept.

When the service ended and they milled through the foyer, Pastor Marshall wasn't at the back, shaking hands as he usually did. Neither was his wife. Come to think of it, where was Pastor Eli?

Emma tugged on Dad's arm. "Do you think Pastor Marshall is okay?"

"What?" Dad looked down at her. "Why wouldn't he be?"

Had no one else noticed? But Josh's grandparents closed the church office door behind them. Mrs. McDiarmid was the church secretary. Something was wrong.

She could ask Josh later, if the grapevine didn't get to her first. Josh's grandmother couldn't keep a secret to save her life.

A little hand tugged on hers, and she looked down into the eager face of Josh's nephew. "Hi, Soren! Did you go to Sunday school today?"

He nodded solemnly then pulled again. "When can I ride a horse, Miss Emma?"

She hesitated, remembering Ian's reaction the other night. Should she offer? "You should ask Uncle Josh. The horses are coming to our place this afternoon."

Too late she recognized Josh's cowboy boots behind his nephew. His jeans. Uh... she raised her eyes. All of him. *Be brave.* "Hey, Josh."

"Hi, Emma. This afternoon, you say?"

"Yeah, we're going out for lunch now." It was on the tip of her tongue to invite him along. *Don't be* that *brave, Emma.* "Dad figured he'd be to Happy Trails with the stock trailer by about four o'clock."

Josh looked down and ruffled his nephew's hair. "I can't remember when I last rode."

Emma kept forgetting not everyone around Jewel Lake had lived on a ranch. "Laire is super calm." She bit her lip. Go for it? Courage seemed overrated. Or was it? "If you want to come around then, we could take a couple of the horses up the trail. Soren could ride with you, if it's okay with his parents."

"Ride with you, Miss Emma?"

She smiled down at the little guy. "Or with me."

Josh cleared his throat. "I'd really like that, if you're sure."

"It would be good to get the horses accustomed to their new trail network. I'm sure Alexia and Vivienne would like to get out a bit, too."

Did Josh's eyes dim a little at that?

No, she read too much into it. Into him.

But he'd kissed her.

There'd been a reason: to shut her up.

"I'll check with Tammy and Ian."

"You've got my number? Shoot me a text and give me a heads-up. Or I can let you know if anything changes."

"That sounds good. Yeah, Noah made sure I had all your numbers since we're all on the same property."

Of course, that was why.

"Emma! Come on. I'm starving!" Alexia called from the open doorway.

"See you later." Emma squeezed the little boy's shoulder and turned away. She'd set herself up for a world of hurt.

Be brave.

Maybe courage was overrated.

Soren pressed hard against the straps of his car seat in his eagerness to see out the side window as Josh rolled into the stable yard. "Where's the horses?"

"Calm down, cowpoke. Remember you have to listen to me. You can't go running at the horses."

"I don't see any horses."

Only because the livestock trailer blocked the stable doors. No doubt Declan and whoever was helping him led the horses directly into their stalls.

Josh could hardly believe Emma's dad — no, Noah's dad — would loan him a horse indefinitely. Even if the mare was old and had seen better days. He parked beside the smithy and undid Soren's straps. He'd gotten to be an old pro at it since Ian's accident. Now, he grabbed Soren by the hand, and they walked to the stable's side door, since the main one on the end was fully occupied.

They came into the alleyway just as Emma led a tall, black horse toward them.

"That horse is so big!" Soren pressed against him.

Emma grinned. "She sure is. You can see a long way from the back of a horse because you're so high up."

"Really?"

"Really. Are you going to ride with me in a little while?"

Soren seemed to shrink. "Maybe I'm scared."

"You can be brave. I won't let you fall." Emma's gaze glanced off Josh's for a second.

Did she mean him, too? It certainly seemed like she might like him a little, but she was afraid. Yikes. That made two of them. He was terrified.

"Keep moving, Emma. I'm right behind you!" Declan roared.

Emma rolled her eyes and turned her horse into a stall.

Declan caught sight of Josh. "Oh, you're here. Let me introduce you to Laire. And who are you, little man?"

"I'm Soren."

Somehow Josh's nephew had found his voice again. "He's my sister Tammy's son."

"Good age to start a boy riding. He probably needs a pony, though. We've got a couple up at Rockstead for the grandkids. You should bring him up sometime to ride with Oakley and Penelope."

"That's a generous offer, sir." One that Josh wouldn't be taking him up on. "Is that Laire you've got now?"

"Laire?" Declan barked out a laugh. "This here is a gelding, boy. Tonto's no mare."

"Oops." So, Josh wasn't up on horse anatomy, though he

certainly knew a stallion when he saw one. Most ranchers preferred not to keep one around since they could be extremely territorial and aggressive. Leave them to the stud farms, one of the ranchers on his circuit had told him.

"Laire's the swayback in the next stall. Take her a carrot. She'll be your best friend for life. You know how to feed her?"

"Flat palm."

Delcan nodded and turned Tonto into his stall. Wait, was that soft murmur the gruff Declan talking sweet nothings to the horse? Josh couldn't help his eyebrows shooting up. The man had many surprises.

"Don't mind my dad," Emma said softly.

"I heard that!" Declan bellowed.

Josh grinned at Emma, and she grinned back before gesturing to the bucket hanging from a hook. "Carrots are in there. Tonto's in the last stall. Then we can saddle up and go for a ride. I'll take him this time, I think."

"Are your sisters coming, too?"

The grin on her face faded. Oh, man, she thought he wanted Alexia along when he really, really didn't.

"Not today. They both had other plans."

"Good."

She studied him for a second but looked away when her dad came out of Tonto's stall, dusting his hands. "I'll leave it to you, then, Emma. You have everything under control?"

"Sure, Dad. Thanks so much."

"Your sisters ought to be here helping you. I trusted all three of you to take equal parts in running this place."

"It will work out. Don't worry about it."

Josh could see why Declan was concerned. Emma seemed to be the only conscientious one of the bunch.

"If you're sure." Declan nodded. "Let me know if Brent's crew doesn't get your plumbing in tomorrow. I'll light a firecracker under his rear."

"It's fine. They're on schedule."

"Okay." He looked between Emma and Josh before tapping Soren on the head twice. "See you later."

Josh held his breath until the click of Declan's boot heels faded away. The man closed the stable door at the far end then the truck started. The sound diminished as he drove away. Then Josh looked at Emma again. "All right. Pretend I'm an absolute newbie, because I basically am."

Emma turned to Soren. "You need to watch from right here. You may not come closer to a horse without a grownup. Do you understand?"

The little guy nodded emphatically.

"Okay. We'll start with Laire. Here's how you tack up a horse."

A few minutes later, they led both horses out into the open corral. She reminded him how to mount up, and he miraculously made it first try. Then she lifted Soren to her own saddle, swung up behind him, and gathered her reins. "Ready?"

Josh settled himself into the leather seat. It was all coming back to him. He fingered Laire's mane. "As ready as I'm going to get."

"I'm ready," Soren announced.

"Good." Emma's knees gently pressed against Tonto's sides. "Walk on."

Laire followed behind with no hesitation, and Josh

relaxed a little more. He urged the mare beside Tonto. Soren's wide grin split his face.

Josh could hardly blame the kid. The sensation of being on a horse again felt euphoric, and to think he could ride this one whenever he wanted. But best of all was riding beside Emma. There weren't many better ways to spend a Sunday afternoon.

Unless kissing was involved.

She'd turned down a repeat. Of course, she had. He'd been a blundering idiot to kiss her like that without an invitation. He'd hoped to convey his interest in her, rather than in her twin, but it hadn't come across that way. Man, he should have kept his mouth to himself that day. He'd made everything all kinds of awkward.

Now he glanced over at Emma again. Truth? His eyes spent more time looking at her than at the trail.

She looked at him, and a flush swept up her fair face. "Beautiful day for a ride."

"It is. You're beautiful, too."

"You don't have to try so hard, Josh."

His eyebrows furrowed. "What am I trying too hard? To tell you I find you attractive? But I do." Josh held his breath.

"I know you prefer my sister."

"Emma?"

She glanced at him then away, but he waited until her gaze returned. "I find you more attractive than Alexia."

"News to me."

It had been news to him, too, but that didn't make it less true. "I figured out that everything I like about your sister, you are the same or more. And you have many excellent qualities she doesn't dream of having. I like you."

Emma bit her lip before leaning over Soren. "Would you like to go faster? Hold on!"

Soren nodded and clung to the saddle horn.

Emma urged Tonto into a lope and took off up the trail.

Josh, too, would like to go faster. And he needed to hold on for the ride.

CHAPTER
Sixteen

E mma couldn't believe he'd said that. Did she simply
look easier to catch than her twin, or what? Argh,
she didn't want to believe that of him, but what
was she supposed to think? Josh had been obsessed with
Alexia for years. He'd never even seemed to notice Emma's
existence until recently, but how could a guy do such a
complete about-face?

He couldn't, that's what. He was playing some sort of
game.

But it didn't seem fair to believe that of him, either. He
seemed to be too honest and open for that sort of guile.
Which then meant he'd changed his mind.

How could she even want the attention of the man
who'd pursued her sister? How pathetic did that make her?
A glance around Creekside Fellowship — or all of Jewel
Lake — didn't reveal any guy who might distract her from
Josh McDiarmid. She'd worked summers at Sweet River
Ranch and met many nice men, but none had caught her
eye. The Timber Framing Plus crew teemed with muscled

guys in their 20s. She enjoyed flirting with Finnley and Xavier, but falling in love with either of them? Puh-leeze, no.

She compared everyone to Josh. How ridiculous.

Unless it wasn't. What if she actually gave him a chance to prove he cared more for her than for Lex? What a glutton for punishment! If Alexia observed Josh noticing Emma, she'd probably want him herself, after all.

Oof. Did Emma really think that poorly of her twin? Alexia wasn't a saboteur. If she said she wasn't interested in Josh, then she wasn't, and she wouldn't try to ruin things for Emma. She might be flighty and thoughtless but not mean. Usually.

"Miss... Emma? It's... so... bouncy."

The little boy in front of her clung to the saddle horn as though his life depended on it.

"Sorry, Soren." She slowed Tonto to a walk. "You didn't like to go fast?"

His head shook against her chest. "It's scary."

"I didn't mean to make you afraid, buddy. I like it when a horse goes fast. It feels like I'm flying like a bird."

"Like a robin?"

"Hmm." Emma couldn't help but grin. "More like an eagle, maybe. Have you seen how they swoop in the sky?"

"Yes?"

"Doesn't it look fun? That's how I feel on a horse." She remembered riding in Jude Kline's helicopter over at Sweet River. It had been exhilarating, but she'd take the back of a horse any day of the week. She preferred a horse between her knees rather than the emptiness of the sky surrounding her.

"I feel more like my teeth will be jolted out of my head."

She hadn't even noticed Josh pulling up beside her. "I'm sorry for running off."

His gaze met hers for more than a second. "I get it. I'm scary."

"No!" Soren insisted. "Horse is scary."

Josh's eyes softened as he looked at his nephew. "I think we'll both start to like it soon. Miss Emma makes it look so easy. I know there's a trick to not bouncing around, but I couldn't quite get the hang of it."

"Were you bracing yourself in the stirrups?"

"Of course. I didn't want to fall off."

"That's the problem, then. You have to go with the flow."

He gave her an incredulous look. "Ever heard of gravity? I'm pretty sure that anything flowing goes downhill."

Emma chuckled. "I thought you'd ridden before."

"Not much, and not for years. In case it isn't obvious."

Oh, it was evident, all right. Why had she assumed? Just because he was a farrier comfortable working around horses on the ground didn't mean he was an experienced rider. "Okay, I failed my first test as a Happy Trails owner, and that's evaluating a client's experience level before turning them loose."

"I didn't fall off." Was that a grin trying to emerge? If so, she'd feel better.

Soren twisted to see his uncle, and Emma's arm automatically tightened around the boy. "I didn't fall off, too."

"Good job, kid." Josh nodded solemnly at his nephew.

The horses stepped onto the top of the knoll, the end of the trail. Emma already knew where she wanted the trail to loop around from here along the other side of the property, but this was it for now. "Want to get down for a few minutes? I brought a snack."

Soren leaned his head back to look at her. "A snack?"

"Uh huh. Cookies and water. Is that okay?"

"I like cookies."

Don't we all. But Emma didn't say that. "Hang on while I get off first, okay? Then I'll lift you down."

Soren nodded, and a minute later, they were all standing on their own two feet. Emma had managed not to watch Josh dismount. She didn't need the visual in her head.

"Does the horsey get water, too?"

Emma shook her head. "Tonto and Laire will be okay until they get back to the stable. I'll make sure they get lots of water and a snack there, okay?"

The little boy nodded. How sweet that he was concerned about the animals. That said a lot about his nature and how Tammy and Ian were raising him.

"Where do I tie Laire?" Josh looked around the barren, rocky hilltop.

"She's trained to ground-tie."

"To what?"

"My brothers have trained all the Rockstead horses to stay put when you drop their reins to the ground." She demonstrated with Tonto's. "He's not going anywhere, even though he's not actually restrained."

"Huh." Josh let Laire's reins touch the rocks. "Just like that?"

"Just like that." Emma shrugged out of her pack and handed them each a bottle of water before opening a baggie of cookies and setting it on a rock. "Sorry. I didn't bake these myself."

"You don't have a kitchen." Josh sat on the ground with Soren crowded against him.

Emma laughed. "Which is why I bought them at the farmers market. I can't wait until everything in my house is finished. I'd hoped it would be before I went back to work, but it's not looking likely at the moment."

"I'm sorry to hear that." Josh took a bite of his cookie. "Not bad, even if you're not the cook." He winked.

He winked.

Did that mean he was flirting? A wink hardly counted after a kiss, no matter how awkward that had been.

Emma looked out across the view of Maranatha Inn, the Christmas tree farm, and the rolling hills beyond.

"What made you decide to become a teacher?"

She glanced at him. "I wanted to be part of forming the next generation to think well and to love learning."

"Ambitious."

Emma shrugged. "I don't know about that. Maybe it was the easiest path, what with my mother and one of my sisters-in-law being teachers. Maybe I didn't think that hard about it. It seemed natural."

"Kids need great role models."

"So, what made you decide to become a farrier?" Especially when he could hardly ride, but she wouldn't throw that in his face. She'd asked him the other day, but he'd deflected then.

"Always fascinated by horses, even though I had few opportunities to be around them. And I like making things with my hands. Also, I'm not that good at school stuff."

"But you like reading, unless that's changed."

"I don't read as much as I used to. Life's busy."

"Blacksmithing is hard work." She'd watched her brother often enough to know those muscles hadn't appeared out of nowhere.

"It is, but it's also creative. Not the horseshoes so much."

She gave him a quizzical look. "I don't mean to sound dumb, but here we are. Horseshoes are what a farrier does."

"Lots of blacksmiths don't shoe horses. And not every farrier makes other things, but I enjoy it."

"Like what?" She might be staring at him now, but whatever.

He shrugged and picked up a small rock, turning it over and over in his hand.

"Like what, Josh?"

"Just random things. Nature-inspired hooks. Candle stands. That sort of thing."

"I want to see!"

"I don't carry them in my pocket."

Well, no. Wrought iron wasn't exactly light as feathers. "Will you show me later?"

"If you want."

"I do want."

He shot her a low look before taking another gulp of water and rising. "I should get Soren back to his parents."

Josh nudged Laire to follow Tonto back toward the stable. The view of Emma's long hair held in place by her cowboy hat before tumbling down her straight back filled his vision. She was beautiful. Strong. Capable.

Had he mentioned beautiful? Because she was.

She kept to a sedate pace on the return trip, yet it seemed no time at all before they rode into the Happy Trails yard. If he'd thought to conjure up the nerve for another conversation, the sight of Vivienne currying a horse in the corral blew that impulse out of his head.

"Hey, guys! Nice ride?" she called.

"Yep." Emma swung down then lifted Soren to the corral's top rail. "Sit tight for a minute."

Josh dismounted, too. "What do I do now?"

"Ground tie her while you go for a brush."

"You mean just let the reins hang down." That still seemed like a crazy idea.

"Yep. Laire's brush will be in her kit bag Dad brought."

"She has her own?"

"Of course."

Of course. Josh had so much to learn about caring for his own mare. Or about this loaner Declan had put into his care. He could only hope he wouldn't do anything terrible to the horse. He wouldn't mean to.

They brushed down the horses in near silence before leading them into their stalls where cool water flowed into their waterers. Josh followed Emma's cue in offering a little grain then watched as she talked to the other horses for a few minutes.

"I ordered a pizza delivery," Vivienne said from behind him. "Sticking around, Josh? There's probably enough."

He shook his head. When he next stayed, it would be on Emma's invitation, not one of her sisters. "I need to get my nephew home."

"I like pizza!"

Josh ruffled the boy's hair. "Not tonight, kid, unless that's what your mom has planned at your house."

Soren's lower lip protruded.

Josh tapped it. "No pouting. Say 'thank you' to Miss Emma for the horseback ride."

"Thank you, Miss Emma."

"You're welcome." She crouched in front of Soren, getting to his level. "Come again another day, okay?"

"Okay." Soren slipped his hand into Josh's. "We can go now."

But Josh didn't want to leave Emma's presence. "Thanks so much. I really enjoyed the ride and learned a lot." Not only about riding Laire, either.

"Sure. Any time." But she didn't meet his eyes. "Hey, Lex."

He hadn't even noticed the third sister's arrival, but now he looked up to see Alexia striding toward them in the stable's alleyway. It would be rude to ignore her. "Hi."

Alexia swept a bow, dramatic as always. "Hello, everyone. Sorry I missed the ride."

She didn't look sorry. "Rides are on your doorstep now whenever you want."

"Once I get moved in, anyway."

Josh had nearly forgotten she wasn't living onsite like Emma. "Well, I gotta go. I told Tammy I'd have Soren home by dinner." He steered the boy past Alexia and out the door where he finally managed a complete inhale for the first time in several minutes. He hadn't said goodbye to Emma, but it would be way too odd to go back for that.

Who was he kidding? Everything about his feelings for her was weird. No wonder she didn't believe his change of heart. He could scarcely believe it himself.

She'd expressed interest in his smithed objects. Would she like a decorative hat rack like the one her dad had commissioned? Josh knew right where it would go in her house. That spot between the front door and the closet just begged for something rustic and beautiful.

Rustic, yes, but were his skill levels up to making it beautiful enough for Emma's gorgeous new home? Her father found Josh's work attractive. Worth paying money for. Josh had only thought of it as doodling with iron before that. He'd been the student who embellished the margins of his exercise books with scribbles of all sorts.

But that spot in Emma's foyer begged for a hat rack. Maybe a freestanding coat rack as well. The design sprang to his mind as he buckled Soren into his seat. He'd have to hold it there until he got back to his apartment where he could draw it out and make sure the reality could meet the vision.

It would be his housewarming gift for Emma.

Would he have to follow that with gifts for her sisters as they moved in during the following weeks? He'd worry about that later. For now, Emma was all that mattered.

Maybe for always.

CHAPTER
Seventeen

B rent! This is amazing." Emma clasped her hands in front of her, unable to stop the beaming smile that covered her face. And why should she?

The contractor grinned at her. "They did turn out pretty nicely. You made good choices."

Several workmen wrestled sections of red alder cabinetry into place in the space that had finally started to take the shape of a kitchen. The appliances remained in their cartons in the garage beside her kayak, having been unboxed just far enough that Brent could confirm they were the correct models and undamaged. But the cupboards came first.

Vivienne came over and slung her arm over Emma's shoulder. "Wow. It's coming together. I hope mine will look as good. Now you have me second-guessing every choice I made for my home."

"Yours will be great, too." Traditional oak wasn't Emma's thing, but her sister obviously preferred the look.

"I hope so. I think it's too late to change my mind."

Brent nodded at Viv. "Now that they've cleared Emma's cabinetry from the shop floor, they're hard at work on yours."

"So… too late."

He chuckled, obviously not taking Vivienne seriously.

Emma wasn't sure she should, either, for all that she didn't want to live with shades of gray and golden oak herself. A lot could be done to brighten up a palette like that. If Vivienne wanted. Emma preferred hers to reflect nature from the base up.

"Where's Lex?" Vivienne asked. "I thought she'd be here."

Emma shook her head. "I think she's hanging out at the stained-glass studio today."

"Is she always like this?" Vivienne scowled thoughtfully. "I know she had a lot of trouble settling on a major—"

"Trouble? She never did."

"Right. But it seems she's into every single form of arts and crafts now."

"Like a honeybee, hovering, dipping, and buzzing off to the next one." It drove Emma crazy.

"Not like a yellow jacket? Your face look like it's fully healed now."

"It's all good." She stopped herself from touching the one on her temple that still sometimes aggravated. But something about the analogy about being bee-like was stuck in her head. Or butterfly-like. The vision of Alexia fluttering from art form to art form seemed to be occluding some reality behind it. Never mind. The reality? Alexia wasn't ready to grow up.

Vivienne kept talking. "I was worried about those stings."

"I knew I'd be okay. I've been stung often growing up."

"Josh seemed so concerned."

Emma shifted on her feet and glanced over at the workmen. Brent measured the gap for the dishwasher as Xavier fastened the sink cabinet into place. No one paid any attention to the sisters' conversation. "I have no clue why he reacted like that. I mean, I wasn't having my best day ever, but I didn't ask to be carried down the hill at full tilt."

"He cares about you."

"Pfft. You're confusing me with Lex."

"I don't think so. He's always watching you."

"He's afraid I'll spontaneously combust after he went to great lengths to save my life."

Vivienne grinned, shaking her head. "Don't be so blind you miss your chance with him. He's for real."

Emma bit her lip and stared at the guys bringing order out of chaos in her kitchen. Turning a shell into a home, but what kind of home would it be without a family to share it with? Josh had definitely looked at her the way Vivienne hinted at but, not long before, he'd been chasing Alexia wholeheartedly.

Had he since then?

Nothing came to mind — which was some sort of relief — but that didn't mean she could trust him.

Vivienne's elbow nudged Emma's side. "Give him a chance."

"He hasn't asked for one. Fine by me."

"He's right there."

Emma almost didn't hear her sister's low words. When

they registered, she swung to face the door, and Vivienne was right. Josh stood just inside with his hands behind his back, his gaze toggling between her and the workmen.

She was the homeowner here. Guess that meant she was in charge of the welcoming committee. "Hey, Josh."

"Hi, Emma! Hi, Vivienne!" His gaze flitted to Viv for a second but then refocused on Emma. "This is looking great."

What, he'd seen the cargo trailer pulled up at the door and decided to investigate? The trailer had often been parked here. Maybe she was being unfair. "I'm happy with what I'm seeing." Oh, man. Talk about leading words. "I mean the cabinetry."

Crinkles formed around his eyes as the only concession to a grin. "I know that's what you meant."

Vivienne snickered quietly. "Gotta go. Catch you later." She excused herself around Josh and disappeared.

Josh came closer, still focused on Emma. "Where are the kittens?"

"Locked into one of the bedrooms. They are not happy in there."

"I thought they were going to be outside cats."

"They will, but not when there are quite this many vehicles coming and going." Though the stable yard would remain a busy area.

"I... uh... I brought something for you. A gift."

"You did?" And why? But Emma managed to leave that unasked.

"Yeah. I know it's not much, and you're not fully settled in, but I thought you might like this over there by the door." He held out a wrought-iron wall rack with half a dozen leaf-shaped hooks on it.

She blinked, unable to resist reaching out to touch the cold metal. "Josh, that is… wow."

"If you don't think it matches your decor, you could hang it in a guest room or a closet or something. Or just say you don't want it."

"Are you kidding me right now? This is stunning. I'll be proud to have it on display. You made it?"

He shuffled from one boot to the other before meeting her gaze for a quick second. "Yeah. It's not perfect. That one leaf isn't on straight. I'm still practicing, but—"

She pressed a finger to his lips to stop the self-deprecating words. "It's beautiful." Then she became aware of the warm sensation of his shaven upper lip against her finger.

Where on earth were her thoughts? But his dark eyes had captured hers, and breathing seemed difficult. She slowly pulled her hand away, willing it to stay out of trouble. Too late, though. It had given her away.

"Emma?" Josh's voice sounded dusky.

"Yes?"

"Would you go out with me?"

"I… maybe?" Who was she kidding? All the way yes, the way he looked at her right then, like no other woman existed.

"Thursday night?"

"Okay." There'd be no sleep for the next couple of nights.

Josh had been quadruple-guessing his plans since he'd asked Pastor Eli for the loan of his canoe. Tammy thought a paddling picnic was the dumbest possible idea for a first date, and Josh couldn't help wondering if his sister might be right.

He'd stopped by Thursday morning to let Emma know to wear casual clothing, sunscreen, and bug spray. She'd looked intrigued but hadn't asked for details.

Now he'd parked in front of her place with a canoe strapped to the racks on his pickup and a cooler in the back. He rang the doorbell — hey, look, it worked! — and waited until she came to the door.

"Hi, Josh." Then her gaze went past him, and her eyes widened. "We're going paddling?"

He gulped. "Only if you want to. We can do something different if you prefer. We can go for a drive or a hike. I have a picnic. We—"

"I love being on the water. Taking kayaks out was one of my favorite perks working at Sweet River Ranch. Even though I have my own, it's been so busy this summer I've barely had a chance."

"Oh." He managed to exhale. "I'm glad. I've always enjoyed it since Pastor Eli used to take the boys camping in youth group."

She grinned. "I was always jealous the girls didn't get to go."

"Well, then. Are you ready?"

"I just need to make sure the kittens have enough food. Come on in for a minute."

The kittens? That sounded like an excuse, but he entered and closed the door. Immediately his eyes found the iron rack he'd made hanging in its intended spot beside the closet. "Hey, you got someone to hang the rack."

"Got someone?" Emma came back around the corner. "I own a drill and a power driver, and I'm not afraid to use them."

Insert foot in mouth. "I should have expected that. It looks good there."

"It does. Thank you. And yeah, don't forget I'm perfectly capable of using power tools. I'm not a simpering female out of some old-fashioned novel."

"I'm sorry."

"Forgiven." She grabbed a sun hat from the hooks. "Do you have life jackets? I'll grab mine from the garage."

"Yes, I borrowed two PFDs from Eli and Harper, but bring yours if you prefer."

"Will do." She tucked her wallet into the pocket of her shorts and zipped it up. "I'm ready."

He ushered her outside and opened the truck door for her before rounding the vehicle. He needed to pay closer attention to his assumptions about her.

It wasn't a long drive to the wharf by the town park, where he parked the truck.

"Need a hand with the canoe?"

"I've got it, but you can bring the paddles and PFDs."

"Okay."

Josh pulled the canoe back until the stern rested on the

pavement before stepping beneath it to set the yoke on his shoulders. It balanced well as he carried it to the water-front and tipped it onto its bottom on the sand. Whew. He hadn't made a fool of himself in front of Emma. Yet.

"I'll grab the cooler and lock up the truck. Be right back."

Emma nodded as she buckled her personal flotation device.

A minute later, Josh set the cooler in place and began pushing the canoe out into the cool lake water. "Hop in?"

Emma rested her paddle across the bow to balance the craft as she climbed in. Handy she'd done this before. Josh waded out a little deeper before clambering in himself. A few strong strokes later, and they headed east along the shoreline.

He closed his eyes for a brief second. *Thank You, God, for nature. For water and trees and mountains.* He could feel the very peace and stillness of the moment sifting over his heart.

Emma twisted slightly to look back at him. "You had no way to know how much being on the water means to me. Here… I feel I can breathe. It's like sitting inside a cathedral."

"That's exactly how I feel. Like all the problems and issues and turmoil drift away. They're not important here. Here it's just me and God. And now you."

"I'm honored to be part of that." She turned to face the front again and dipped her paddle into the calm lake water.

Huh. Josh guided the canoe toward one of his favorite pullouts where he'd often camped as a teen.

"Look!" Emma said in a low voice, her paddle pointing nearly straight ahead.

Josh leaned to see past her where a vee formed in the water behind a moving brown head. "Beaver?"

"I think so. Let's get closer."

They paddled synchronously and silently to meet the mammal. They weren't noticed until they were within a canoe length. With a mighty flip, the beaver slapped its tail on the water and dove.

"So cool." Emma glanced back at him, her face glowing in the late afternoon sunshine. "At Sweet River, I often snuck up on loons just at sunset. It was like a game to see how close I could get."

How had Josh ever thought Emma insignificant? She was the best possible match for him in so many ways. Their journey together had only just begun, and he could hardly wait to participate in the rest of it.

Emma Cavanagh had his heart. He'd been blind to the reality, but he could see it so clearly now. Could see *her* clearly, and not just the Emma who sat straight and strong a few feet ahead of him in Eli's canoe, but the woman who was stalwart in every other way, as well.

Now he just needed to not mess things up.

CHAPTER
Eighteen

E mma settled on a log and watched as Josh kindled a fire close to the water's edge. How could he have guessed what a perfect date might look like to her? She hadn't pulled the green-and-alder palette out of a hat. The colors of nature soothed her heart.

She loved water, true, but somehow blues had felt too chilly to surround her in her home. She loved the choices she'd made, and this moment reminded her why.

The flames caught on the handful of twigs Josh had placed on a blackened flat rock, and he fed a few thicker pieces in until they, too, blazed. A moment later, he sat back on his heels, apparently satisfied with his efforts.

Then his gaze locked on hers, and it felt like that little fire sucked up all the oxygen for miles around. How long had she waited for him to truly notice her? Since high school, not that she'd held any hope. She'd dated some in college and left a string of *just friends* behind. She hadn't really connected with any of them.

Was Josh it for her? Last month, he'd chased Lex. But

that had been then, and this was now. The way he looked at her did not make her feel like a consolation prize nor like a means to make her twin jealous.

It looked real.

But could it be? Josh's interest seemed as fickle as Alexia's romp through the arts.

But it wasn't. He hadn't dated half a dozen girls this summer, and Lex had dabbled in at least that many art forms in that amount of time. Why wouldn't she settle?

Also, why allow distracted thoughts on the perfect date?

"I'm glad you're here," Josh said simply.

"Me, too. Thanks for inviting me."

He came around the flames to sit beside her, only a hairsbreadth between them. She could feel the heat of his thigh and arm next to hers.

"I know we don't need a fire to keep warm, but it just sets the ambience for a picnic."

"I agree. I love a campfire." He'd picked a good spot for it, too. They'd paddle away knowing they left no embers behind that could start a wildfire.

The sun angled low in the sky across the lake, casting a golden glow over everything. A family of ducks swam around the rocky point nearby, and a lone loon called from somewhere in the distance.

Peace.

Then Josh's leg brushed hers, and the flames seemed to leap from the campfire into the spot where they'd touched. She looked up at him. So near. And he looked at her like he'd never seen her before. Which seemed fair, given their history.

"Hungry?"

Oh, yeah. But he meant food. "What did you bring?"

"I stopped at the diner. I wanted to fix something myself, but I chickened out." He hesitated. "I'm not that great of a cook."

"I worked as chef's helper the past few summers at Sweet River Ranch. I'm kind of looking forward to cooking now that my kitchen is all set up." Brent's crew had been working on the tile backsplashes for the past couple of days and had hooked up the sink and dishwasher earlier this afternoon. The fridge and range might be in place when she got home.

"I bet you're a good cook."

Emma shrugged. "I learned some tricks from my boss. I can make mean sourdough bread! But I'm not sure that's practical for one person."

"I'm jealous. Fresh bread is a luxury item."

"Yeah, I agree. If I make some, I'll slip you a loaf."

"I'll hold you to that." His stomach rumbled, and he laughed as he patted it. "Now my body thinks I'm getting fragrant, fresh bread right now, but it's wrong. I'll grab the food."

He ambled over to the canoe and removed the cooler, which he set beside a rock. A few minutes later, he'd spread a cloth and laid out a container of sandwiches and another of salads along with a bottle of sparkling water and a couple of tumblers. "There's dessert, too, but shall we get started?"

What an adorable grin.

Emma rose and skirted the fire to get to where he stood.

He held out both hands.

She blinked but took them.

"Dear Lord, thank You for today. Thank You that we can enjoy the beautiful creation You have made. Please bless our time together and this good food. In Jesus's name, amen."

"Thanks," she whispered. That might have been one of the negatives with the guys she'd dated in college. Even the believers hadn't led with grace over their meals. If her heart needed any more melting, this prayer might have done it.

Josh still gripped her hands. "Thanks to you, too, Emma. I'm so glad you're here with me."

She dared a peek at his face. "Me, too."

The moment held, but just when she wondered if he'd lean in for a kiss, he let go of her hands and turned away, clearing his throat. "Here, let me serve you. Estelle sent ham sandwiches and egg salad. I like them both, so choose which you prefer."

"I like both, too." Emma still reeled. What had almost happened there?

"Then we'll split them." Josh still didn't look at her. "There is bean salad, coleslaw, and potato salad. Preferences there?"

"I like them all, so I'll have a little of each."

Not quite meeting her eyes, he shot her a quick grin. "You're easy."

Hopefully, not *too* easy. "I'll try to be pickier in the future." She reached down for a plate just as he did, and their heads bumped.

"Sorry." Josh pulled away. "Ladies first."

What had happened to that moment? Had she imagined that they'd had one? She couldn't have. He'd definitely held her hands for prayer and longer. "Okay." She put a little of everything on her plate. Hopefully, her belly wouldn't rebel because her appetite had fled.

"Everything at the Golden Grill is so delicious." Emma reclaimed her spot on the log. "I didn't know they did picnics to go, though."

"I ordered everything a couple of days ago, so Estelle and Leo had time to pull it together."

"That was very thoughtful of you."

Josh looked across the little beach at her. "Thanks. I wanted everything to be perfect, but then I second-guessed everything. I don't know how to attract a woman."

"By being yourself?"

"That…" His voice petered off.

Emma nearly kicked herself. Being himself hadn't worked with Alexia. Now, she shoved her twin right out of her head once again. "Just be yourself, and the right person will find that attractive. I guess that's what I wanted to say."

"Thanks. I'm sorry. I feel so awkward."

Were they going to have to address the elephant in the room? Perhaps. "Do you still have a thing for my sister?"

"What?" Josh started. "No."

"Do you… have a thing for me?" *Way to be brave, Emma.* But she didn't feel brave.

"I do. But yeah, you had a front-row seat to my obsession with Alexia, and that's embarrassing. I feel like that high-school kid all over again."

"That was six years ago. I don't think you're still him."

Heaven only knew how much Emma had matured in that interval.

"You don't?"

"Well, bits of him remain, but that's as it should be. I…" She should not divulge this, but her voice plunged on ahead of the caution in her brain. "I thought the teenage Joshua McDiarmid seemed pretty cool."

Josh stared at Emma. Had he really heard her say what he thought she'd said? "You liked me in high school?"

She bit her lip. "Yeah?"

"Whoa. I never knew." Somehow his wooden legs returned him to the spot beside Emma. He lowered himself to the log, careful to keep some air flowing between them. Her revelation required some thought. He'd had no clue. He'd just felt like the scrawny, mouthy boy no one wanted. What could she possibly have seen in him back then?

"I think that sums up high school." Emma laughed, but not like she found it funny. "I liked you, but you liked Alexia, and she liked—"

"Danny. And Danny liked Shelby." Josh glanced at Emma. "A whole string of unrequited crushes."

"Teens, huh?" Looking down, she turned the plastic fork over in her hand.

Josh nudged his elbow against hers. "I'm honored you saw anything worthwhile in that kid."

Emma's gaze flew to meet his. "Why would you say

that? You were athletic and got decent grades and were..." Her face flushed.

"Were?"

"Kinda cute."

Her voice had quieted so much he barely heard it. "You thought I was cute?" How had he never figured this out back then? What kind of oblivious guy kept focused on someone who clearly didn't want him when someone as amazing as Emma had?

"Yeah." She elbowed him back and straightened a little. "But don't let it go to your head."

"I'll try. But I seriously had no idea."

"Need I say it? Teenage boys are clueless. It's a well-documented fact."

"You're probably right. Okay, wow. So, we wasted like six years."

Emma glanced his way. "I don't think it was a waste. We've each found our path in life since then. Grown up a bit... hopefully, a lot. Besides, how many teen crushes turn into something lasting?"

He studied her profile as she took a bite of her ham sandwich. "Not only pretty, but wise."

She arched a brow at him. "Don't forget surprising."

Whatever reluctance she'd shown a few minutes ago, she'd obviously overcome. Had it been his assertion that he really, truly, had overcome his crush on Alexia?

Josh pressed against her shoulder. "I don't think I could forget that if I tried, but now I'm curious. You can handle power tools. What else should I be warned about?"

"Hmm." She swallowed her bite. "Depends on what

your preconceived notions are. You already know I'm the youngest of nine kids…"

"You're a twin."

"And Lex is older by eight minutes, which no one in my family has ever forgotten. Even Vivienne, and she wasn't even around back then. But it means I had to fight for everything. Dad only cared about his sons back then."

"They split up, and you moved to town with your mother."

"Right. Dad didn't even fight for us."

"Wasn't it the best thing for you?" He wouldn't have really known either twin if they hadn't shown up in Creekside Academy sophomore year.

"Yes, but Dad… never mind. He's changed. He's a different person now."

"Six older brothers. I can hardly imagine. There was just Tammy and me and a step-sibling here and there, depending on who my dad was with at the time."

"That must have been rough." She eyed him.

"At times, yeah. If it weren't for my grandparents, I don't know what would have become of us."

"That reminds me. I saw them follow Pastor Marshall into his office after church. His face looked kind of gray. Do you know anything?"

She meant because Grandma couldn't keep a secret if her life depended on it. At least, this didn't fall into confidential territory as far as Josh knew. "My grandmother said Pastor Marshall nearly collapsed. He was supposed to go on vacation in September, but I think the board is sending him and his wife early."

"I hope he comes back refreshed. I enjoy his ministry."

Josh nodded. "I can relate more to when Pastor Eli preaches. I think Pastor Marshall must be nearing retirement. I wonder if that means the church will call Pastor Eli as the lead pastor? I hate to think of the next generation of teens not getting his full attention the way we did."

"Plus the Pot of Gold hunt every summer. Would he have time to do that if he oversaw all the ministries?"

"I don't know. That geocaching event has become so big, I'd hate to see it sidelined." Josh shook his head with a chuckle. "I guess this proves we're adults now, looking at the future of the church we call home."

"We should be praying for the church leadership as well as Pastor Marshall's health. Is your grandma doing okay? She had that heart attack years ago."

"As far as I know. It slowed her down some, though. She cared for my nephews the day Tammy helped with the trail, and she called in sick to work the next day. She was just exhausted. Tammy felt terrible about it, but Grandma had insisted she wanted to help. I guess those days are behind us now."

Which meant his grandmother would likely never babysit Josh's own kids. The kids that weren't even a gleam in his eye yet. Although, he could *almost* see a little girl and boy living in those two spare bedrooms in Emma's house. It had the makings of a real family home.

Josh blinked. Yeah, leaping from crush to full-blown crazy had been his nemesis in the past. He needed to take it step-by-step with Emma and not let his longing for a more stable family than he'd ever had push him into being too hasty.

Did that mean putting off kissing Emma again? He'd

certainly rushed the first one, and he wouldn't make that mistake again.

She'd admitted she liked him in high school. Admitted she liked him now. When would he know the time was right?

Caution had better be his middle name for the foreseeable future. Joshua Caution McDiarmid.

CHAPTER
Nineteen

"Did Josh kiss you?"

"No." Had she wanted him to? Kind of. It would have had to be better than the first attempt, but what if Josh were stringing her along? She didn't *think* he was, but how could she be sure? How could she trust him? And if she let herself kiss him back, he'd know how much she cared. She'd be too vulnerable.

"Good." Vivienne sounded smug.

Emma shot her sister a glance, but she seemed focused on spreading fresh sawdust in Tonto's stall. They'd fallen into a good system over the past few days with more horses in the stable. Even Alexia did her share before disappearing for hours on end.

An engine cut out in the yard, and Emma dusted her hands on her jeans before heading out to see who'd arrived. Not Josh's truck or Noah's. She knew the sounds of those.

"Who's here?" Vivienne asked.

"I'm not sure." They'd run an ad in the Jewel Lake

Gazette that had garnered several phone calls and email inquiries. Maybe someone had decided to check out the facilities in person.

Emma squinted into the morning sun as a man exited the low-slung sports car that screamed of money. It also screamed of a city boy.

"Hey, Emma! Long time no see."

She blinked. "Branson DeWitt? Is that you?"

"In the flesh." He held out his arms.

Emma dashed into them and gave him a squeeze before stepping back. It had been several years at least since she'd seen her brother Ryder's best friend. "Wow, I didn't know you were back in town. Or are you just visiting? Have you seen Ryder yet?"

"I'm opening a law office here. I had dinner with Ryder and Carey last night."

"We can use an ethical lawyer in town." She grinned up at him. "I assume you qualify, anyway?"

"Very funny." Branson's gaze went past her toward the stable, and he blinked.

Emma glanced over to see her sister leaning against the doorframe, arms crossed.

"Vivienne?" Branson appraised her with an appreciative smile. "Wow, you're looking good."

Emma noted that he hadn't said that to her, not that she would have expected it. She'd been Ryder's bratty little sister last she'd seen him. There was an eight-year age gap between Ryder and her.

"Branson." Viv's voice dripped icicles.

Emma's gaze swiveled between them. They knew each

other? Branson hadn't been around much after he'd gone off to college... before Vivienne had entered their life.

Branson tucked his hands in the pockets of his dress slacks and rocked on his heels. Not cowboy boots, but polished Oxfords. He didn't look like a Jewel Lake resident, but Emma wasn't about to give him style tips.

"Nice place you've got here. I hear you're ready for business?"

Emma narrowed her gaze at him. "Yes, at least partially. We have a few horses available for trail rides, but lessons won't start until September." If Alexia followed through. "We also have some stalls available for boarding horses."

He nodded. "That's what I'd like. A place to keep Franklin close to Agate Bay so I can ride him often."

"You have a horse?"

"Of course."

Of course, nothing. Not the way he was dressed.

"Ryder said I could keep him up at Rockstead, but that's a long way out of town. This is under five minutes from my house, so I'll be able to ride more often."

"Um, sure. The boarding rates are on our website."

"I looked them up, and the terms are agreeable. I'd like to fill out the paperwork and bring Franklin by on the weekend. He's still with my buddy near Great Falls."

"Okay. Viv?" Emma turned to the stable door, but her sister had disappeared. So much for asking her to deal with the forms she'd created. "Never mind. Come on into the office, and I'll get you set up. Since you'd be our first boarding client, you can choose Franklin's stall. I should also mention that we offer farrier service onsite, but if you have a different one you prefer, it's not against our terms." She led the way as she prattled on.

"Noah's the best farrier around. I'm happy to have him in charge of Franklin's shoes."

"Noah's apprentice, Josh McDiarmid, is our resident farrier."

"McDiarmid? Familiar name, but I can't place him."

"His grandmother is the secretary at Creekside Fellowship."

Branson snapped his fingers. "Ah. Right."

Did Branson still attend church? He and Ryder had been in youth group together, but that didn't mean anything anymore. She hadn't really kept up with her brothers' friends. Vivienne was nowhere to be seen when Emma and Branson toured the box stalls.

Branson pointed out the vacant stall next to Tonto's. "It might be easiest for you if they're grouped together."

"Sure. We do expect to be full soon, and then it won't make any difference, but it's a fine choice, regardless."

They entered the open office area, and Emma rummaged for a paper application. Viv thought everything should be electronic and had set up the online form, but apparently, Branson was a hands-on kind of guy. She attached the papers to a clipboard and handed it to him. "Unless you want to take it home then drop it back later?"

"Now's fine. I think I have all the information with me. I don't have a local veterinarian, so I'm good with whoever will be around to care for your horses."

They needed guest chairs. Emma made a mental note to add that to their official shopping list as she gestured to the tall stool behind the desk. "Make yourself comfortable."

Branson nodded, bent his head over the clipboard, and began to fill in the blanks with a neat hand.

Now what? Where had Vivienne gone? Emma looked out into the corral to see her sister with her arms wrapped around Nightingale's head. The sight would be heart-warming if the timing didn't seem odd.

Was Vivienne avoiding Branson for a reason?

Josh pulled up beside the smithy at Happy Trails. One decided disadvantage of Emma living on the premises was he couldn't tell if she were at the stable or not, because she never drove over. But there was a car, a red Ferrari. Only flashy money drove that kind of car.

Should he wander into the stable and see if Emma was in there? He couldn't wait to see her, to see how she'd react to him after their date last night.

It had taken all his self-discipline not to kiss her. He nearly had at the picnic, and again when they pulled in at the marina, and again when he left her on the doorstep. Had she wanted him to? He couldn't read her, and the memory of that ill-timed kiss a couple of weeks ago lingered. No, he had to know for sure it's what she wanted as much as he did.

Josh glanced between the smithy's locked door and the stable's open one. Emma was likely over there, though it might be one of her sisters. He could take the chance and open the shop five minutes from now. Nothing would be the worse for wear.

But he'd only taken two steps across the parking lot when Emma exited the stable, a guy dressed in a suit right behind her. The man slung his arm over her shoulder, and she looked up at him, laughing.

Josh's boots stopped moving, nearly pitching him face-first to the ground. Was this what it felt like to be attacked by a pack of yellow jackets? Because there seemed to be buzzing all around his head, stalling his thought process.

Who was that guy? More importantly, how did he know Emma? Because she seemed awfully glad to see him for someone who'd claimed to enjoy a date with Josh just last night.

She wasn't a two-timer. Not Emma.

But, well, evidence.

Emma caught Josh staring and smiled. Waved. Turned back to the man, who slid into the Ferrari. She leaned against his open window for a minute before stepping back. The car revved its way down the drive, and Emma stood watching until it disappeared before she came toward Josh. "Hi!"

"Who was that?" Sheesh, he sounded jealous. Bitter. Maybe because that's how he felt.

"The guy who just left?" She angled her head, studying him.

"Yes. Mr. Fancy Pants."

Emma laughed. "Branson DeWitt. Do you remember him? He and my brother Ryder were buddies as teens."

"The name isn't familiar."

"Yeah, those guys have eight years on us."

Did Emma prefer older men? Maybe someone who clearly had money like her family? Josh did not fit that bill. He was the same age as her, plus her brother's apprentice. His family lived hand-to-mouth. If a red sports car could turn Emma's head, she wouldn't remain impressed with Josh. That is, if she even was now.

"Bran's going to be stabling his horse here. Our first boarder! He's just moved back to Jewel Lake to open a law office."

More and more information Josh didn't want to know. And also, she'd shortened the guy's name. They were obviously on close terms. The arm over her shoulders, the smile they'd shared, had already told him that.

And Josh seethed with jealousy, a mix of anger and fear and the memory of never being good enough. Which was all kinds of crazy.

Emma studied him. "Are you okay?"

Josh gave his head a quick shake. "I... I think so. Just, are you seeing him?"

"*Branson*?" Her voice sounded incredulous.

"Mr. Fancy Pants."

"Didn't I tell you he's my brother's friend? I haven't seen him since... man, I don't even know when. I think I might have run into him a couple of times since Ryder and Carey's wedding, but he's not really on my radar, so I'm not sure."

"You're not interested in him?"

"No." She eyed Josh. "You're jealous."

"Me? No way." He grimaced at his flat-out lie. "But seeing you so cozy with him kind of got to me. I mean, I know we've just gone out once. We haven't made any promises to each other."

Emma's eyebrows tipped up. She crossed her arms and tapped her cowboy boot as she studied him.

He couldn't take his gaze off her. She might be small, but her expression and stance were both on the intimidating side. She was still beautiful.

"You really are jealous."

He gulped. "Maybe? A bit." More than a bit. The amount astounded him, honestly.

"I like that look on you." Emma's mouth quirked upward on one side. "Makes me think you're over my sister."

Josh latched onto her gaze. "I am definitely over your sister."

"Good." She glanced over her shoulder, moved a little closer, and lowered her voice. "Here's something curious, though. Viv totally disappeared while Branson was here. She's usually so professional and polite, but not with him. I didn't even know they knew each other. But something must have happened between them in the past."

"Huh." Josh didn't much care about Vivienne's love life or lack thereof. Thankfully, she'd been right there treating Emma's stings that day, but otherwise, he'd barely registered her existence.

"I had fun last night, Josh. Thank you."

The buzz from his... okay, fine, call it jealousy... dissolved and floated away. "I did, too." He hadn't dated a ton, but taking a girl canoeing wouldn't have been in his file of date ideas before seeing the kayak racks on Emma's truck. He'd taken a chance — against Tammy's fervent advice — and won.

Now he stood in front of Emma, debating what was next. "We should do it again. Or maybe something else. Are you free Sunday afternoon?"

Her face twisted. "No. I've got a family thing."

"Okay." He couldn't expect her to invite him so soon. Could he handle the scrutiny of all Emma's brothers as her date? Yikes. He'd be okay with Noah, but Travis and Blake, especially, were intimidating. Adam, Nathaniel, and Ryder would likely link arms with the others in creating a formidable gauntlet for Josh to run before he could be accepted. What was he thinking, dating a woman with six older brothers?

That she was a great girl.

That he liked her a lot.

That her father didn't seem to mind him. Declan had given him his wife's mare. Or loaned her to Josh. One or the other. But that had been as Noah's apprentice, not as Emma's boyfriend.

Was he her boyfriend? Was the designation too high school?

"I'll be back here by early evening, if you want to come over. We could put on a movie or something. I haven't gone shopping for furniture yet, but I do have a TV and a bunch of pillows."

Josh grinned with relief. "And you have kittens."

"I have tiny attack beasts with teeth and claws."

"You love it."

Emma chuckled. "I do. They're crazy wild things but great company, all the same."

"That sounds like a perfect evening."

"It's a date, then."

Date number two. Josh could live with that.

CHAPTER

Twenty

Y ou could have stayed and caught a ride with someone else."

Like whom? Emma scowled at her sister, who descended the ranch road with considerably more speed than generally recommended. "No one else is going back to town later, so you're my ride." She'd often come up with Viv on Sundays, and this was the first time the decision had bitten her backside.

Vivienne shrugged. "I'm sure someone would give you a lift, or you could stay over and come down with Noah tomorrow. I could have checked the kittens and horses tonight."

A girl couldn't argue with Vivienne when she got obstinate like this. Emma opened her phone. She would only have a minute to send a text as they flew past the cell booster beside their brothers' homes halfway down the mountain.

Lex, tell everyone Viv and I aren't coming. We were all the way to the top when Viv remembered she has to set stuff up at the clinic for tomorrow's immunization event, so we turned around. Have an extra burger for me!

Emma's finger poised over the send arrow, waiting for the final curve when cell bars would magically appear.

"Don't be angry with me."

She turned to glare at Vivienne again. "I am angry. You're not usually disorganized, so I have to assume your sudden recall had to do with seeing Branson's car at Mom and Dad's."

"I *said*, I have to set up for the clinic." Vivienne's jaw set.

"Sure, you do."

Aha. They were within range of the booster. Emma hit 'send' on the text. A few seconds later, Alexia replied.

Alexia: *Viv actually forgot something?*

Yeah, Emma's thoughts exactly.

Alexia: *Drive up yourself?*

Emma: *Takes too long by the time I get back.*

And they were out of cell signal again. Rockstead lay a solid half hour from the east side of Jewel Lake, and Happy Trails lay on the west side. By the time she got back up there in her own truck, lunch would long be over and the babies napping. Sure, Dad would grill another burger for her, and Mom would pull the leftovers out of the fridge. They might even wait dessert for her.

She'd be starving to death by then, and she really didn't want to make a scene, either on her own account or trying to explain Vivienne's actions to the family. No, she'd take a rare Sunday afternoon for herself. Too bad she'd told Josh she had unalterable plans. Too bad Vivienne hadn't received the memo herself.

"You're mad at me."

"Yeah, I am."

"Look, I'm sorry."

"You could explain, because I know it has nothing to do with work."

"It does so."

"Fine." Emma stared out the side window the remainder of the bitterly silent trip to the highway.

They drove past the scenic viewpoint overlooking the town and the lake, then wove through the streets leading to the Agate Bay subdivision. Finally, Vivienne pulled up in front of Emma's house. "I'm sorry."

"Save it." Emma jumped out and shut the car door.

Vivienne glared at her as she turned the car and sped away.

Everything she did was perfect. No matter what Vivienne said, there was exactly a zero-percent chance she needed to be at the clinic right this minute, and a one-hundred-percent chance she was avoiding Branson DeWitt.

Emma had simply been a casualty of the skirmish, an innocent bystander caught in the crossfire.

Her phone had been pinging with messages as they drove through town, but she'd been too angry with her sister to accept the distraction. Now she sat on her shaded stoop and looked at the messages.

Mom: *I'm so sorry you and Viv couldn't make it.*

Emma rolled her eyes. That's exactly what had happened.

Ryder: *Aw, I was looking forward to reintroducing Viv to Bran.*

Oh, Ry. That ship had well and truly sailed. Good to

know her brother was just as oblivious as Emma had been. Which meant whatever had gone down, Branson hadn't confided in Ryder. Because something *had* to have gone down.

Lex: *I would have brought you back down. I'm planning to come later, anyway.*

Now Alexia told her? It would have been useful information earlier.

Emma had an entire afternoon to herself. She could go for a ride on Desiree or work on lesson plans, though those were all but complete since school would resume in just a week. Or she could do something else, like unpack boxes.

Her stomach growled. Start with lunch, then. She'd counted on one of Dad's juicy burgers, and nothing in her brand-new fridge would come anywhere close. A visit to the Golden Grill would be the first item on her agenda.

Josh's hammer rang out as he beat a piece of red-hot iron into the shape of an eagle feather. It needed to be a similar size and style as the others, but not identical. As though identical were even possible.

He swiped at his sweaty face with the sleeve of his denim shirt. Smithing was brutal in the heat of summer. He usually worked his creative pieces early in the morning, but he couldn't ignore a free Sunday afternoon.

Horses were great. He did enjoy farrier work, but there wasn't a lot of room for creativity within the bounds of a perfectly fit horseshoe. But this? Seeing something in his mind and turning it into reality with his own sweat and muscle? Satisfying in a way a flawless horseshoe couldn't be.

Last year, he'd gone to an art show in Spokane. One booth had really stood out to him, though the man hadn't been a blacksmith but a welder who created gorgeous, detailed sculptures out of all kinds of random junk and found objects. He'd told Josh he had pieces in art galleries all across the west.

Wesley Ferguson had become Josh's new hero, though the man had no idea how much inspiration he'd exuded.

Josh had never thought of himself as artistic. Sure, he'd doodled in the margins of his school notebooks. Didn't everyone? But oils and acrylics and watercolors held little appeal. Any pictures he attempted to paint refused to reveal what he saw in his mind.

Smithing, though? Somehow, beating iron into submission seemed easier — not physically, but with more satisfying results.

It also gave him time to think, not always a good thing. Today, he mulled on Pastor Eli's sermon. He'd picked up the series Pastor Marshall had been preaching about boldness, and Josh had to wonder if he was that kind of godly bold or whether he was just impulsive and brash.

Only a guy with some sort of misplaced confidence would ask out a girl he hadn't seen in six years. No wonder Alexia had turned him down, but hadn't that turned out for the best? Because she'd helped him see how much more perfect her twin was for him. She'd been right. Emma was amazing, and he could hardly wait to hang out with her this evening.

Scriptural boldness was different, though. It relied on a sure foundation of knowing what God wanted, and knowing the Holy Spirit would provide the conclusion.

Josh hummed "Standing on the Promises," an old hymn they'd sung before the benediction today. One of the verses had stuck in his mind.

Standing on the promises that cannot fail, when the howling storms of doubt and fear assail; by the living Word of God I shall prevail, standing on the promises of God.

He'd never taken much of a stand. His grandmother had seen to it that he attended Sunday school and youth group and even Creekside Academy, the private school associated with the church where she worked. He'd accepted Jesus as a young teen, but had he ever really taken a stand? Ever stepped out in boldness?

Eli had preached on David. Of course, Josh had heard the tale of David and Goliath since he'd been knee-high to a flat rock. The shepherd boy had taken a big risk he'd be able to kill the giant with only his sling, and God had honored his faith. That was how Josh remembered the tale.

But he'd heard it differently this morning, and it made sense. David hadn't been naively brash and hopeful. He hadn't really taken much of a gamble stepping out. David knew his skill with his slingshot. When everyone, including the king, talked about the armies of Saul, David knew Goliath's contempt had been directed at the army of God. It wasn't Israel being insulted and taunted here, but God.

David merely did what he knew how to do — accurately sling a rock to the spot where it would do the most damage and take down the giant who'd turned everyone else into trembling wusses. They'd forgotten God. David hadn't.

God honored David's boldness. He prevailed.

Josh hadn't faced any giants. No one was threatening the freedom of his people. He hadn't faced an existential crisis in his life, but that didn't mean he couldn't be bold for Christ. What would that even look like to a young farrier in Montana? No idea.

David hadn't known he'd be called on to slay a giant when he got up that morning. When he'd practiced with his slingshot over the years, he'd been focused on protecting his father's sheep from lions and bears. But that had prepared him for the moment when his skill — not luck and not naive hope — could save his people. David was prepared, and this was his moment.

Standing on the promises of Christ the Lord; bound to Him eternally by love's strong cord; overcoming daily with the Spirit's sword, standing on the promises of God.

Overcoming daily. That's what Josh needed to do right now. He couldn't stand on promises he didn't know or understand, could he? Noah had invited him to a men's group Monday nights at the church, but Josh had declined. All those guys were older than him. Most were married and had kids.

But Josh needed friends and mentors. Would it be so bad if these guys had already walked some of the paths Josh hadn't?

He'd go on Monday.

Now for another forged feather.

Emma sat curled up against Josh. The closing credits rolled on the big screen when she heard Alexia's truck stop outside. A moment later there was a tap at the door half a second before it opened.

"Hey, are you home?"

Alexia needed to be taught some boundaries. On the other hand, not knowing when Alexia would pop in might help keep Emma on the straight and narrow, not that she had any intention of allowing things to get out of hand with Josh.

"Oh! Sorry." Alexia's eyes widened, but that didn't stop her from coming in and shutting the door behind her.

With Josh's truck parked right outside, she couldn't be ignorant of what she was walking into.

"Hey, Lex." So much for the goodnight kiss Emma had been hoping for from Josh.

"Hey, you two." Alexia smirked. "What have you got for pop in the fridge, Em?"

"Seriously? You come down off the mountain, drive past a grocery store and three gas stations, to see what's in *my* fridge? Nice try."

Josh had already shifted away enough that Emma felt cool air where he'd been pressed to her side a minute earlier. The mood was well and truly shattered. And that didn't make Emma feel much sympathy for her sister.

"Yes?" Lex's voice echoed from inside the fridge. "Why don't you have pop?"

"Because I don't drink it? As you might recall."

"Right. I forgot they brainwashed you against sugar up at Sweet River." Alexia turned, leaned her backside against the peninsula, and crossed her arms in front of her.

They hadn't really lived together in years. Sharing a cabin at the ranch had been more like two ships passing in the night. Emma could almost buy that Alexia didn't know. Almost, but not quite. This whole situation stank like rotten fish.

"I wanted to check on you and Viv, but her car isn't at her apartment or at the clinic."

"She's a grownup." Also, there were phones.

"A grownup who's acting weird."

Emma surged to her feet. Now who was weird? Maybe if she kicked her twin out quickly enough, she could salvage the evening. She and Josh had had such a good time watching an old Western, eating popcorn, and giving each other furtive, flirty glances.

But as soon as she stood upright, her bladder pressed uncomfortably. She paused beside her twin. "Get out of here," she whispered hoarsely. "Don't you have enough sense not to interrupt a date?"

Alexia simply smirked.

Emma pivoted and headed into the master bedroom with the bathroom beyond. Besides peeing, maybe she should take a minute to regain her composure. Honestly, sisters. Who needed them? Both of hers had let her down today.

She patted cool water on her face and headed back

through her darkened bedroom. She'd left the door ajar, and she could hear Alexia's voice in the great room.

"Nice move, Joshy. Way to go after my sister."

Emma's feet gripped the wooden floor. What on earth?

"Thanks for pointing me her direction, Lex. It's working out well."

It was almost like being amid that swarm of yellow jackets again with all the buzzing. With all the stinging. With that sense of disorientation. Josh had literally swept her off her feet in that moment.

Now, it felt like he'd dropped her to the hard, rocky ground.

CHAPTER
Twenty-One

Emma held her head high as she re-entered the great room, though her entire body vibrated in anger and frustration.

Alexia stood where she had been, leaning on the island, while Josh stood a few feet away, hands in his pockets. Alexia smirked when she spotted Emma. Yeah, they knew each other's tell-tale signs. They knew the buttons to push for maximum reactions, and Alexia was pushing one now.

Emma had put up with her twin long enough. She pointed a finger at Alexia. "You may leave. Now."

"Me?" Alexia looked confused. Surprised, even.

"You." No way she didn't know what she'd done wrong, but maybe she hadn't realized what Emma had overheard. Hadn't figured it out.

Alexia exchanged a glance with Josh.

Emma turned to him. "You may also leave now." Keeping her voice firm and even was the hardest thing she'd done in ages.

He took a step toward her, one hand stretched toward her. "Emma?"

She backed up. "Now."

"What's wrong?"

Emma's eyebrows shot up. "You have got to be kidding me." Who knew a soundtrack of buzzing accompanied the red haze of anger? Maybe Dad did. He'd had massive fits of rage back in the day before he'd made things right with God and Mom and the family.

She would not lose control like Dad had done. She would not. Her fingernails bit into her palms as she clenched her fists to her sides, and she welcomed the pain, not that it diverted her attention from the agony in her heart.

She'd been played.

Well and truly played.

She had no one to blame but herself. She'd doubted that Josh could turn so quickly from Alexia to her, but he'd convinced her that his feelings for her were real.

Ha, ha. Big joke, and it was on her. Alexia and Josh were laughing behind their hands right now, though Lex's smirk had wiped away. Josh, however, was a better actor than she'd suspected, because his eyes looked troubled and sad. His whole posture was turned toward her, not Alexia.

Had he been in any of her drama classes in high school? If not, he'd wasted a golden opportunity. He could pretend to be anything at all, and people would believe him.

Emma had lapped it up, but she was wiser now. Better now than later, when she'd really fallen in love with him or something stupid like that.

Okay, she maybe already had, because she'd been

primed for years to like him. Sliding deeper hadn't taken much. It would have been as hard to avoid as escaping Pompeii upon the eruption of Mount Vesuvius.

She had the bruises on her heart to prove that the volcano had smothered her. How long would it take those to heal? Would they ever? She had no idea.

Emma lifted her chin and stared Josh down. "The door is over there."

He looked helplessly between her and Alexia. "Can we talk about this — whatever *this* is — tomorrow?"

"I don't think so."

"I don't understand."

"Think about it… on your own time."

"Emma." His voice was suffused with confusion and longing.

Nope. She stood firm.

Actor. Player.

After a long, unflinching moment, he turned and headed for the door. It closed behind him, then his truck engine started, then the sound of it dwindled.

Emma bent down to pick up Tangle, who'd been twining around her ankles. At least she could trust in the love of her cats. People — even her first friend, her twin sister — were completely, one-hundred-percent untrustworthy.

She stared at her sister, who hadn't so much as twitched. "Why are you still here?"

"Why are you so angry?"

"Nice move, Joshy. Way to go after my sister," she mimicked then switched to imitate Josh's voice. "Thanks for pointing me her direction, Lex. It's working out well."

If Alexia had any sensitivity at all, she'd be cringing in the corner by now, shielding her face and her kidneys. But, of course, no.

Alexia sighed and shook her head. "Twinnie, hasn't life taught you not to jump to conclusions?"

"No, actually, it hasn't. Life has taught me to trust my instincts." Which she absolutely had not done in regard to Josh.

"Oh, I thought you were going to preach me a little sermon about life teaching you to trust God instead of leaning on your own understanding. You know, like in Proverbs."

"Don't even try to turn this conversation into something it's not. This isn't about God. It's about my backstabbing sister."

"Puh-leeze."

"So, you told Josh to go for me, huh? Why? So you could laugh at how gullible I am?"

Alexia's eyebrows rose. "Anything else you'd like to accuse me of?"

"Are you telling me that I misunderstood that little exchange? What else could the two of you been discussing, I wonder?" She couldn't have mixed those signals. Could she?

"Context, sweet sister, is everything."

"The context is that you knowingly interrupted my date with Josh in my own home and, when you thought I wouldn't overhear you, complimented him on making me fall for him."

"Did it work?"

The only thing within reach to throw at her sister was

the cat in her arms, and poor Tangle didn't deserve a ten-foot flight. Even if she would land with all 18 claws ready to pierce Alexia's skin. Emma clenched the kitten tight. She couldn't ever remember being this angry before. Calm, cool, and collected Emma, the mature, polite twin, had been taken over by a raging demon.

For good reason.

Was any reason good enough?

Shush.

"Look, Josh likes you."

"You expect me to believe that after all this?"

"He probably likes you a little less for kicking him out of your house like a raving lunatic."

Emma stalked a few steps closer. "And how would you be privy to that information if you two hadn't talked about me behind my back?"

Alexia shrugged a single shoulder as though she hadn't a care in the world. "I'm not denying we talked about you."

"Get out."

Lex eyed her. "I don't think so. I brought my sleeping bag to stay over. I'm meeting with a stained-glass artist at seven in the morning, and Happy Trails is a lot closer than Rockstead. I'm not driving back."

Emma was supposed to care about that? "Camp at your own place."

"Without indoor plumbing? I don't think so."

"Go away. Stay with Viv." But even Emma could hear the resignation in her tone. A person could hold onto fury so long before it gutted and exhausted her.

"I'm not going anywhere until tomorrow morning, Em." Alexia sauntered into the great room, snagged the nearly empty popcorn bowl, and picked out a few kernels. "Yum. What seasoning is on this?"

Emma spun on her heel, stalked into her bedroom, then shut and locked her door. She threw herself across her bed while sobs rolled out of her innermost being.

She'd trusted Josh. She'd trusted Alexia. Neither of them deserved it.

The grief was real.

Josh paced his small apartment. What had happened? Emma was furious with Alexia for interrupting their date. He got that. He hadn't been any too pleased himself when she strolled in like she owned the place.

He'd been looking forward to the right moment to talk to Emma about kissing. After that first ill-timed event, he knew he needed to hear her words of acceptance. He'd been hoping for eagerness, actually. Or maybe for her to take the reins and get things started herself. He'd have happily gone along with it.

But she'd stepped out of the room and come back like a raging inferno.

Why?

Nothing could have happened in her bedroom or bathroom. All the cats had been in the great room.

She'd come back snapping. Shaking.

Josh stared out the window. He couldn't see the lake from here, but his apartment did have a view of Creekside

Park beside the church. Nothing to see there but a couple of lamp posts beside the path, puddling circles of light amid darkness.

Darkness. He felt it to the depths of his soul.

What were the lamps? What held back the darkness right now?

God.

This morning's sermon about David's boldness and confidence had seemed such an encouragement earlier. Now, it was empty. David had been a guy who lived thousands of years ago. He'd killed a giant. Ho, hum.

What did that event have to do with the life of Joshua McDiarmid halfway around the world 3000-ish years later?

God hadn't changed, though. He was the same yesterday, today, and forever.

Josh wasn't an Israelite, one of God's chosen people.

Not a good argument, either. Hadn't St. Peter said to the gentile church, 'you are a chosen people'?

Josh pivoted for his phone and looked it up in his Bible app. There. 1 Peter 2:9-10. *For you are a chosen people. You are royal priests, a holy nation, God's very own possession. As a result, you can show others the goodness of God, for he called you out of the darkness into his wonderful light.*

He might not be an Israelite, but he'd been chosen. He poked around the app a little more before discovering Ephesians 1. *Even before he made the world, God loved us and chose us in Christ to be holy and without fault in his eyes. God decided in advance to adopt us into his own family by bringing us to himself through Jesus Christ. This is what he wanted to do, and it brought him great pleasure.*

Okay, so maybe David's experience with God was valid. David had been bold and confident because of two things. He'd known his own skill and ability... and he'd known God's.

Still didn't explain what had gone down with Emma, though.

He and Alexia had been talking by the kitchen island when Emma returned...

He and Alexia had been talking...

Josh smacked his forehead.

They'd been talking about Emma. Just a few words, but had she overheard? Had she jumped to conclusions? Because what he'd said to Alexia had been genuine. He'd thanked her for helping him to truly see her sister. To see Emma. He'd thanked her because he meant it. He was thankful for Emma.

Had he sounded insincere?

What impression had Emma received?

He closed his eyes, cringing. She'd obviously received the wrong one, and why? Because he really had been an idiot. He'd set himself up for this by pursuing Alexia on a whim after not seeing either sister for years. Emma had even questioned if he could truly have a change of heart and like her more than her sister.

He'd insisted he only saw her. Emma.

She'd finally come to accept his words as truth, but her misgivings must have still been present beneath it all.

Josh had needed more than a week or two to flood her with so much attention that the old foundation would be completely washed away as no longer relevant.

The phone in his hand dinged with an incoming text.

Emma?

His heart surged in his chest as he looked down then sank at the sight of Alexia's name.

Alexia: *She's mad because she thinks we're laughing at her behind her back.*

Josh scowled at his phone. How could Emma think that? Not after the fun, low-key evening they'd had.

Josh: *You shouldn't have barged in like that.*

Alexia: *Yeah, apparently true. Sorry.*

But he'd responded to what she said when Emma was out of the room. He hadn't said anything wrong. Not really. But his words of gratitude had been ill-timed. Or maybe he hadn't said enough. Instead of saying it was working out well, he should have said how much he liked being with Emma. Should have admitted his actual feelings.

But no. He hadn't really acknowledged them to Emma yet. Telling Alexia first would have been stupid.

Even more stupid than the conversation she *had* overheard?

If only Alexia'd had the smarts to stay away. If only she hadn't said anything leading about his relationship with her twin. If only...

But it had happened.

Emma had kicked him out of her house instead of kissing him goodnight.

He had no one else to blame but himself.

This was going to be a sleepless night, but he knew how he needed to spend it. Back to the words of St. Peter: *Humble yourselves under the mighty power of God, and at the right time he will lift you up in honor. Give all your worries and cares to God, for he cares about you.*

Being lifted in honor might not mean winning Emma back. The most important part was humbling himself before God. Giving over all his worries and fears.

God cared about Josh McDiarmid.

He cared about Emma Cavanagh, too.

Alexia, even.

Please, Lord, work everything out to Your good. Help me to want Your best more than I want Emma.

CHAPTER
Twenty-Two

No one would even know Josh had been here if he didn't enter the church doors. He'd walked over, since he lived only two blocks away, but now that he stood on the edge of the parking lot and saw all the vehicles, he wasn't so sure.

He counted three Rockstead trucks, but that didn't mean all six of Emma's brothers weren't present. They lived far enough out of town they probably carpooled. And didn't Emma know all the guys from Sweet River, since she'd worked there in recent summers? That probably made them additional big brothers, as though the Cavanaghs weren't enough.

There'd be a few other guys, too. Probably all married.

Josh was a failure at relationships. He'd feel like a little kid playing basketball with the big boys. They'd indulge him — even pass him the ball once in a while or hold him high so he could make a basket — but he wouldn't be part of the team.

Be bold.

Wasn't that what he'd been learning from the David story? Not a bluffing, hope-for-the-best brashness, but a boldness rooted in confidence in God.

But Josh wasn't good at that part, either. He did way too much relying on his own instincts and not nearly enough depending on God. Which was why he'd come here.

It was 6:58. He either needed to man up or slink home in defeat.

Be bold.

That suited guys like David. Like Moses and the Apostle Paul. Like Josh's biblical namesake, Joshua.

Yet all of those Bible heroes had failed. The men inside Creekside Fellowship had, too. Humans tended to do that. Josh was not alone in defeat... but it wasn't defeat if he didn't give up. Then it was merely a setback.

A car careened into the parking lot and squealed to a stop. Kirk Kennedy jumped out then seemed to notice Josh. "Hey! Coming in?"

Josh straightened his shoulders. "Yep."

"Great! How's the trail building going over at the stables?"

"Uh... good, I think. They've staked out a second route."

The man grinned. "The community needs this. If Lyssa and I were living here full-time, we'd get a horse for the kids and board it at Happy Trails. But alas, we're still in Butte through the school year for a while longer."

Right. Kirk taught at U of M over there, and Lyssa taught school. Third grade? Josh couldn't remember. In the summers, they lived in the gatehouse at his brother Dale's lakeside property here. Together, Kirk and Dale owned Communication Location in downtown Jewel Lake.

Kirk pulled the church door open and ushered Josh inside.

He was here now. Josh inhaled. Exhaled. Braced himself for the onslaught of Cavanaghs. Did any of them know he and Emma had been dating? Noah did, but Josh hadn't seen his boss since Friday. Had Noah heard about yesterday's collapse of civilization?

Josh preceded Kirk to the fireside room on the lower level where the men sat in a large, loose circle.

"Hey, look what I found outside!" Kirk slung his arm over Josh's shoulder. "You all know Josh McDiarmid, right? Josh, the guys."

Josh managed a grin and small wave. There were only a couple he didn't recognize. He hadn't hung around the Sullivan bunch from Sweet River but knew most of them on sight.

"There's a seat over here, Josh." Noah pointed at the armchair beside him.

"Thanks." Right in the midst of all of Emma's brothers. Great. Josh nodded to those nearby.

"Let's get started," Pastor Eli said from over by the fireplace, which was thankfully unlit on this August evening. "Can I get someone to open in prayer?"

"Sure." One of the Sullivan men — Tate? They kind of ran together in Josh's mind — ducked his head. "Father God, thank You for this group of guys. I pray that You'll bless our evening together. Give Eli Your words as he leads us tonight, and challenge us all to be the leaders and men you've called us to be. In Jesus's name, amen."

Josh wasn't leading anyone anywhere, and after yesterday's bumble, he felt more like a toddler in a man's body.

But to be a man, he had to step into the role. Accept it. Accept responsibility for his words and actions.

He'd texted Emma an apology, and she had not replied.

He'd driven into Sisters Close, but her truck had not been parked there. She still didn't have a garage door, so she couldn't hide her vehicle.

Now, he had to wait. And, possibly, use his time wisely to figure out how God could grow him through this situation.

"Hey, Eli, how is Pastor Marshall?" Blake Cavanagh called out.

Eli shook his head. "The doctors are running some tests, so we don't know anything until results are back. Meanwhile, he's taking some personal time off. Hopefully, he'll be back in the saddle before too long."

"Are you doing all the preaching in the meanwhile?" Maxwell Sullivan wanted to know.

"I am, unless one of you wants to volunteer? Or I could really use some help with the youth group over the next few weeks. We've got the kickoff stuff for the new school year coming up, too. It's a busy season around here, and not when Marshall or I usually choose to take a vacation."

Noah shifted in the seat beside Josh. "I could do things with the youth if you point me in the right direction." He glanced at Josh. "Wanna help?"

"I… uh…" Everyone in the room seemed to be looking at Josh. "So long as you're in charge, not me." He didn't have much of anything else to do on his Friday nights right now with Emma not speaking to him. Did Noah know? Josh didn't want to ask him, especially not in this group.

"Oh, man, I can't thank you enough. Harper's been

worried I'll run myself ragged. She'll be really grateful to you as well. Now, any volunteers to preach in the next couple of weeks?

Uneasy laughter rippled around the room as the guys looked at each other. Helping Noah with the teens was a whole lot easier than preaching, and Josh was off the hook. Whew.

"Ryder, how about you?"

"Me?" The youngest Cavanagh brother blinked as he thumbed his chest. "I've never done any public speaking. I think you've got the wrong cowboy."

"Pray on it." Eli grinned. "Okay, so we're going to take yesterday morning's text from 1 Samuel 17 and dig deeper. It's not that I didn't have time to pick a new passage, in case you were wondering. I mean, I *didn't* have time, but I'd already planned to get in the trenches with you guys and David tonight. That whole concept of boldness is totally based on God's ability, not our own. Let's dig in."

The school year began with a couple of half-days, each with a chapel assembly. As a student, Emma had hated the slow start. She'd always been eager to dive into the new material and put the lonely summer behind her. In high school, she'd lived in town with Mom and Alexia, and didn't even have the option of horseback riding every day unless one of her brothers offered a ride back and forth.

As a teacher, the slower start gave her a chance to get to

know the students a little better and introduce them to how she ran her classes. It still seemed strange to sit with her mother and her sister-in-law Dafne in the back row during assembly. Cavanagh strong.

Priscilla Cantrell, the principal of Creekside Academy, commanded the attention of the assembly as she outlined the academic calendar to the student body. They'd had a staff meeting Monday morning, and Emma had met the newest additions to the teaching roster. Mr. Winslow had finally retired from teaching high-school science after years of threatening to and had been replaced by a middle-aged man from Bozeman, Grant Simmons.

There'd been a rumor they were hiring a younger, single man in that role. Emma could only be glad they hadn't. Josh might be persona non grata, but that didn't mean she wanted anyone else. She'd had a crush on him for too long to be easily diverted.

Pastor Eli offered a short devotional and prayer for the beginning of the school year. "Please pray for Pastor Marshall, kids. He's taking a bit of time off because of his health. You can pray for me, too." Eli chuckled. "Creekside Fellowship is a big church for a small town, and there's plenty going on, so there's suddenly a lot of extra things for me to do. But God knows that, right?"

The students murmured agreement.

"You high-schoolers will be happy to know that Noah Cavanagh and Josh McDiarmid will be taking over the youth group for a while. They're planning a campout on Labor Day weekend. Come on Friday night to hear the details and sign up. Spur of the moment, but that's sometimes how we roll."

Emma gave her mom a quizzical glance. Mom shrugged to say this was also the first she'd heard of it. Right. Noah was a grownup. Why would he consult the parental units over helping at the church?

And Josh. Why would he volunteer? Likely, Noah had roped his apprentice in. But Josh would be good with the teens. He loved all the outdoorsy stuff they'd done in youth group back then.

So did she.

Dafne poked Emma with her elbow. "And that's a wrap."

Oh. The room shimmered with anticipation as the students and teachers rose to their feet.

"You okay?" Dafne studied her. "Your mind seems to be elsewhere."

"I'm fine." Emma had to be. The kids were swarming to their homerooms, and she needed to get her head in the game.

"Talk later?"

"Sure." Was Emma about to confide in her brother Blake's wife? If anyone could understand falling for a player, it would be Dafne. Blake had been a mess when they met, dating three women at the same time. He'd been so full of himself that he hadn't even tried to keep it a secret. Dafne had taken him down a peg or two, and then God got a hold of him.

God could work miracles and turn wishy-washy guys into godly ones. Blake might still think he was the funniest dude on the planet, but he was actually pretty decent now. Solid dad for Dafne's son, Gavin, and for the two younger kids God had given them.

Maybe God could work miracles in Josh, too. Maybe

He'd already started, since Josh had agreed to help with the youth group.

Maybe only Emma was a fraidy-cat, trying to protect herself.

She joined the throng in the corridor as they all headed to their classrooms.

"Ms. Emma?"

She looked down at the girl eyeing her eagerly. "Yes? Maggie Johannesson, isn't it?"

"Yes! That's me. Did you know I don't have a mom?"

"I did know." That sort of information about their students was really helpful.

"I want one really bad. Would you go on a date with my dad? Maybe you could be my new mom."

Wow. She'd never been proposed to via proxy by a middle-schooler before. "I don't think so, honey. Are you in my homeroom?"

"Yeah!" Maggie seemed undeterred. "I think you're going to be my favorite teacher. You live really close to my gruncle's house."

"Your... what?"

Maggie rolled her eyes. "Great uncle is too long to say, so he's my Gruncle Monte. Get it?"

"I get it. Monte Newman is your... gruncle?" Monte's parents — Maggie's great-grandparents, apparently — had been the original owners of the property where the new Maranatha Inn and Happy Trails had been built recently. Monte had retained the parcel of land where his house stood.

"Yep, that's him! He says you're going to have lots of horses. Can I come riding?"

"That will be up to your parents. I mean, your dad." Too late, Emma realized she'd fallen into the girl's trap.

"Okay. I'll talk to Dad. We used to live at my grandma's house, but since she married my grandpa, Dad and I got our own place. But I miss having a mom."

So many questions arose out of that, but Emma didn't know where to start asking them. She'd only get in deeper if she did.

The buzzer sounded. Saved by the bell.

"Time for homeroom!" she announced.

A group of sixth-graders were already milling around the classroom. She needed to put Josh — and the unknown-but-single Mr. Johannesson — out of her mind and start inputting a love for English Literature into the impressionable young minds in front of her.

CHAPTER
Twenty-Three

J osh, right?" The man in front of him extended his hand.

Josh shook it. "Yes, sir."

"I'm Garrett. Garrett Morrison. My parents used to own Canyon Crossing back in the day. I remember when Noah used to be our farrier and come around here on his circuit."

"Noah's a great guy. He's trained me well."

"I'm sure he has." Garrett propped a boot in the rail fence and leaned his elbows on the top. "It's like old times seeing that farrier truck pulled up right here with the mobile forge in action."

"I've been doing the route on my own since spring."

"You've got a bit of the wanderlust, do you? I was surprised when Noah quit most of the circuit a few years ago."

"I believe that was when he married Taryn."

Garrett chuckled. "A good woman has that effect on a man. Makes him want to stick around closer to home."

Josh managed a short laugh. "You must be married."

"I am. My wife's name is Tori. You?"

"Me? No. I'm only 25."

"Hey, don't knock it. A lot of men are married by then. When you meet the right girl, don't let your age slow you down any."

"I might have blown it with her already."

"Oh?" Garrett's eyebrows tilted up as he studied Josh. "You're a Christian, right?"

"I am. Maybe not that good of one, but—"

Josh literally spoke to the raised hand.

Garrett shook his head slowly. "You know following Jesus isn't about *you* being good. It's about Jesus being good."

"Right. I do know that."

"She's either the right woman for you, or she's not. You can only determine that by prayer and patience."

"I'm not so keen on patience."

Garrett laughed. "Who is? Man, not me, either. But it's my wife who was the patient one. She liked me for ages before I really noticed her. Not because I was so great. Trust me on that. I had a huge chip on my shoulder from — well, it's a long story. Either way, I didn't see myself as a guy worth loving. I knew Jesus loved me, but a beautiful, desirable, God-fearing woman? That was harder to believe."

"I get it." Hadn't Emma once said she'd liked him in high school? She'd been patient... but Josh had handled her heart poorly.

"I'm not here to give you advice on your love life. In fact, I didn't come by to talk with you at all but to have a coffee with Noela and Ross. They bought us out years ago now. But when I saw you setting up out here, God gave me a shove to come talk to you."

Josh eyed the older man skeptically. "God does that?"

"Absolutely. I didn't know what He wanted me to talk about. Maybe I haven't found it yet."

"Or maybe you did. You said you were slow to notice your wife. What did it take?"

"A couple of things. One, she left Saddle Springs to go work for Noah's father. She was filling in as a companion to Declan's teenage daughters. Two—"

"Seriously?" What were the odds?

"About what?" Garrett eyed him, obviously confused.

"The Cavanagh twins."

"Yes? The girls spent a few days with Tori at the Flying Horseshoe, her family's guest ranch. Then she went to Rockstead with them for a while. I thought I'd lose her to one of those rugged brothers."

"It's Emma," Josh blurted.

"It's Emma what?"

"That I blew it with."

"But isn't Emma like 14?"

"She was... ten years ago."

"Are you kidding me right now?" Garrett blinked and shook his head. "Time flies. Wow."

"I first knew them in high school. I had a crush on Alexia, but she liked another guy. I had no clue Emma liked me. I was just a scrawny kid with a big mouth back then."

Garrett threw back his head and belted out a laugh. "Oh, Josh. Most of us guys were that kid back then."

"You?"

"Trust me. Or I could show you photos of my adolescence. Anyway, you were saying."

"I met them again a few months ago. Reverted to my teen self and asked Alexia out. True to form, she turned me down. After a while, she clued me in to notice her sister. And she was right. Emma and I dated for a few weeks, and it was going really well. I couldn't remember why I'd ever liked Alexia more when she doesn't have half the depth Emma does. Emma is not only pretty, but she's kind and hardworking and always helping other people. She's amazing."

"I hear a but coming."

"Yeah, Emma found out that I asked her out after Alexia pointed me in her direction. She'd already mistrusted my change of heart. Now she can't see past that."

Garrett emitted a low whistle. "You blew it, Josh."

Way to make a guy feel even grungier than pond scum. "I know."

"What are you going to do?"

Josh shook his head. "I don't know. That happened Sunday evening, and we're only on Wednesday now. I've been praying for guidance, but I really don't know if God has anything for Emma and me, or if I just had a huge, devastating lesson to learn." He grunted. "Me and my big mouth."

"Prayer is a huge first step. Don't underestimate it. Is there any way you can prove to Emma beyond doubt that you love her, not her sister?" Garrett chuckled. "I still can't believe those twins are adults now."

"Emma is definitely a grown woman. She just started

her second year teaching middle-grade English at our church's academy."

"A teacher? No way. My wife is a teacher, too. You gotta watch those intellectual types, Josh. They're deep thinkers." Garrett leaned closer. "Deep feelers, too. You need to speak her language."

What was Emma's language? Besides English Lit. Besides horses.

How could Josh figure out how to speak to her on a level that proved his devotion? It wouldn't be a one-time thing. He knew that. He wanted to communicate with her for the rest of their lives. He was falling in love with Emma Cavanagh.

What was he going to do about it?

He'd think and pray about that while he shod the Canyon Crossing horses.

"Tammy! Nice to see you." Emma pulled her shopping cart to the side of the Super One produce aisle. Not a lie. Josh might be nothing but confusion in her mind, but his sister wasn't part of the problem.

Was Tammy part of the solution? No way to know.

"Hi, Emma."

"No boys today?"

"My grandmother is watching them for an hour. It's killing Ian that he can't manage two little kids on his own."

"Aw, I'm so sorry. His leg isn't getting better, then?"

"Not very quickly. He's grappling with the realization that he's unlikely to return to logging, and that's all he's done. Know of any jobs that don't require mobility?"

Emma heard the barely veiled sarcasm in Tammy's tone, but that didn't mean the question wasn't real. "Hmm. He could step into a pastoral role! With Pastor Marshall's health up in the air, I'm sure Eli could use some help."

"Seriously? That's what you've got? Ian's a great guy, but I can't see him preaching."

Emma totally could, but convincing Tammy wasn't her job. "Visitation? Leading study groups?"

Tammy shook her head. "He can't even drive himself around, and I have no clue when that will be an option. He's totally reliant on me, and our income is suffering. I don't know what we're going to do."

Emma glanced into Tammy's cart and noted the no-name-brand noodles and canned veggies that brought the Phillipses' needs into focus. "Let me think about it. I know a lot of people."

"I know it's not your problem to solve, but thanks. I'll accept prayers, for sure. It's hard on weeks like this when Josh is in Saddle Springs."

Emma had wondered if Josh was avoiding her when she didn't see his truck at the smithy. Nice to know that wasn't the case.

"Hey, I saw the hat rack he made for you. Isn't he talented?"

"He really is. It's gorgeous." Even though he'd made her angry, Emma had to acknowledge his talent.

"He's got an entire closet full of wrought iron stuff he's made."

Emma blinked. "He what?"

"He's been tinkering for the past year or so. He's got hat racks and candle stands and fireplace accessories and who knows what all. I found his stash by accident when I was looking for a roll of paper towels in his apartment. But the entire hall closet was heaped high with a jumble of wrought iron."

"I had no idea."

"He lacks confidence, I think, though everything I saw looked great to me. I don't know why he hasn't tried to sell the stuff. People would go for it, wouldn't they?"

Emma's brain spun. "Yes. I think they would. He should talk to Eryn Sullivan at Sweet River Ranch. She runs the gift shop up there, and she's always looking for local artisans. She has all kinds of crafty things, and tourists snap them up like crazy."

Tammy's face fell. "No one has room or weight allowance to stick iron in their suitcases."

"People who vacation at Sweet River aren't generally on a tight budget. A minor inconvenience like paying for freight isn't a big deal to most of them." Emma shrugged. "And plenty of them drive."

"You'll have to talk to Josh about it."

"Not me." Emma raised both hands. "I'm not the one who knows about his stash. That's you." Also, she'd cut him out of her life. Had that been premature? But he'd hurt her. He'd conspired with Alexia behind Emma's back. Totally unacceptable, right?

The Josh chapter had been forever closed.

He'd broken her trust and made her look like a fool.

The unforgivable sin.

But was it really? After she'd refused to pick up his calls, he'd texted a lengthy apology. He hadn't pretended he and Alexia hadn't talked. He'd acknowledged it but then gone on to say how much Emma meant to him. He'd stopped short of saying he loved her, because of course, he couldn't possibly love her in such a short time.

Emma had loved Josh for a long time.

No, that hadn't been love. Love was real. Deeper. A bond that welded hearts together. Or maybe she'd read too many romance novels.

"When Josh gets back, I'll tell him to invite you over to our place for dinner one night when I'm not working. Ian and I want to get to know you better."

He hadn't told his sister about the breakup. Did that mean he thought it was just a bump in the road? Or maybe he hadn't had a chance before leaving for Saddle Springs.

Emma didn't peek in Tammy's buggy again, but she didn't need to. The Phillipses could barely afford to feed themselves, never mind visitors. If she and Josh went over for dinner — a monumental if — Emma needed to find a way to ease the financial burden a bit.

Could she find a bigger way to do that? Why wasn't Tammy's grandmother arranging a benefit of some sort? Mrs. McDiarmid worked as the church secretary. She had resources at her fingertips. Maybe she thought it would be considered nepotism. Or she'd been distracted by Pastor Marshall's illness. Possibly she hadn't even thought of it.

Emma would swing by the church office after school tomorrow and chat with the older woman. Mrs. McDiarmid was known to be a gossip, and all Emma didn't need was for her to get wind of Emma's failed relationship with

Josh. The entire church — probably all of Jewel Lake — would be privy to the details in no time flat.

It was almost enough to make Emma reject the notion of a fundraiser. But Ian and Tammy's situation wouldn't improve without some intervention. They needed money. They needed help. They needed to know their community would surround them and care for them.

And Emma knew how to take care of people. She'd get something rolling and step back, out of sight.

Because she didn't want Josh to think she was getting involved with his family to make amends with him. The anger still stung. Still hurt.

Would the time come to set that aside? Maybe someday, but she couldn't see it anytime in the near future.

CHAPTER
Twenty-Four

Had Josh ever been this much of a know-it-all brat? He cringed, remembering he'd admitted as much to that man in Saddle Springs a few days back. Now he was surrounded by a pack of teen boys in various stages of puberty, all vying for the basketball.

Noah was little help. The guy couldn't sink a basket if his life depended on it, but whatever. Noah would bring the devotional after Josh had worn the kids out.

There were over a dozen guys and only three girls, one of whom was in the game with her elbows ready to fend off anyone who threatened her possession of the ball. The other two watched from the sidelines, whispering and watching the boys.

Also, they seemed to be speculating about Josh. Ugh. He didn't want the attention of girls that young.

He wanted Emma.

And he wanted the basketball. Taller than most of the

kids, he leaped to catch it. With a twist in midair, he sent the ball spinning toward the basket. Whoosh.

He accepted the hand slaps from his team members as the girl, Maya, laid up her own shot. She was pretty good, to say nothing of brave to join in the guys' game. She reminded Josh a little of Emma, who just got in and got dirty when she wanted something, convention be hanged.

Noah called the group to order, and everyone grabbed bottles of water and sank onto the grass in the shade.

Josh had done his part of the job. Noah was better suited to teach these impressionable teens how to live for the Lord. Josh wasn't that good at it himself.

"Before we get started, I want to talk to you guys about our overnight camping trip on the Labor Day weekend. We don't have enough canoes for everyone to paddle in, so instead of leaving from the dock here, most of us will drive around the lake and hike the last bit to the campsite. Josh and a couple of volunteers will bring most of the gear in the canoes and meet everyone else there. So, if you have a strong preference for paddling versus hiking, you should mention that now."

A couple of the guys waved. Maya raised her hand but lowered it again.

"Maya, you have some experience with a canoe? Steven? Manuel?"

All three nodded. Looked like they'd be Josh's team, then. He could live with that.

Noah continued to outline the activities they'd be doing together, from paddling to swimming to a nature scavenger hunt to talks about God's creation and care.

"Is there going to be a female chaperone?" one of the girls asked. "My dad won't let me come if there isn't."

Noah nodded. "My wife, Taryn, will be along for you girls."

"Okay."

Once Josh had wondered if Emma might volunteer, but the question had never come up. When he'd been a teen, Pastor Eli had only taken a few boys at a time. It had never been a co-ed youth group activity.

Josh had loved the smaller group and the personal attention. Most of his growth as a young believer could be attributed to trips like this one. He'd do his best to help these kids have a meaningful weekend. That meant setting thoughts of Emma aside and focusing on the teens.

But his brain still contemplated how best to reach Emma and show how much he cared. He was still trying to avoid the use of the word 'love' even in his own head, but what was love between a man and a woman if not what had begun to grow between him and Emma?

Josh forced his mind to Noah, who sat cross-legged with his Bible open on his lap. No woolgathering. This job was too important.

"You guys all know Pastor Marshall is sick, which is why Pastor Eli has taken more of the church duties, which is why Josh and I are here with you. When we agreed to take this on, we signed up until Christmas. By then, we'll hopefully have a better grasp on Pastor Marshall's health and the whole situation."

"My family prays for Pastor Marshall at breakfast every day," Manuel said.

Noah nodded. "He and his wife need our prayers, for

sure. Anyway, Josh and I talked over our plans for this fall with Pastor Eli and laid out some goals and plans."

A couple of kids groaned.

Josh couldn't help grinning. Teens were the same now as ten years ago. Anything that smacked of organization reminded them of school.

"Tonight, I want to talk about God's love. Now I think you guys all know about that. Your parents have taught you. You've been in Sunday school since you were toddlers. Many of you are students at the academy and have a Bible class twice a week and chapel on Friday. So, the idea that God loves you isn't exactly news. But we're still gonna talk about it, because love is a hard concept to really understand."

Noah wasn't kidding right now. If Josh couldn't figure out love with Emma, how could he ever understand God's?

"First thing, we can't earn love. Not human love and not God's, either. Romans 5:8 tells us that God showed His great love for us by sending Christ to die for us while we were still sinners. We'd done nothing to deserve that gift. We never could. Totally impossible."

Was the same thing true with human love? Could a person earn that? Hmm. Probably not. One could earn gratitude, but love lived in a different dimension.

"Even acting despicably can't turn love on or off. I hear parents love their kids even if the kids have totally rebelled and cut off contact. I'm not a parent, so I can't speak to that side of it any more than the rest of you. And I know some of you have rough relationships with your parents and might think they don't love you."

Josh thought of his own father. Rough was one way to describe it.

"But that's humans for you. Our love is far from perfect. Some people don't seem capable of loving anyone but themselves. Everyone else's emotions — including their kids' — are just a casualty to making sure Number One is taken care of."

Noah studied the teens. The teens stared back. Josh plucked a piece of grass and shredded it between his fingers.

"God is not like us." Noah's words dropped into the silence. "His love is perfect. It's not dependent on us, which is totally good news, because that means we can't possibly screw up enough to turn His love off. Love, true love, doesn't operate on a switch. It's not like a faucet: on, then off. No matter who we are, no matter what we've done, no matter whether we want it or not, God still loves us."

Josh knew that. He'd known it for years, but something about Noah's quiet-yet-forceful words lodged in a vulnerable spot deep inside. God's love was as firm as bedrock. Nothing could shake it. No earthquakes or volcanoes or tsunamis or wildfires could change the shape of it.

"First John 4 says, 'God showed us how much he loved us by sending his one and only Son into the world so that we might have eternal life through him. This is real love — not that we loved God, but that he loved us and sent his Son as a sacrifice to take away our sins. Dear friends, since God loved us that much, we surely ought to love each other.'"

Noah closed the Bible on his lap and looked around the group. "I'm gonna leave it right there today. Think about that kind of love this week. Think what a different world we'd live in if we all practiced loving like God loves us. Okay? I'm gonna ask Josh to close in prayer and then let you go. Check the church website for the signup link for the campout. You've got until Wednesday to get that in. Josh?"

Noah had asked in advance. Praying out loud had never been easy, but Josh was stepping up as a leader, as a man. He could do this and be a good example.

"I've been thinking." Emma looked between her two sisters sitting on her back deck.

Alexia groaned and threw up her hands. "My worst nightmare come true."

It had taken a few days before the twins had regained their familiar relationship. Maybe it had even improved since Alexia had sincerely apologized for interfering. At least, it had sounded genuine.

Emma eyed Vivienne. "Anything you want to add to Lex's response?"

Vivienne shook her head. "I'm curious what you've been considering."

Emma was so tempted to take the moment to ambush her sister about the thing with Branson, but there'd be time enough for that later. "Okay, you guys know Tammy and Ian Phillips. Josh's sister and brother-in-law."

"Yeah." Alexia grimaced. "That accident was really rough. Is he any closer to going back to work?"

"Between us three, he mightn't ever be able to do his former job. He was a logger, and they need to be super agile to stay safe. It doesn't sound like he'll regain complete mobility."

"Ugh." Alexia wrinkled her nose.

"Injuries like his are rough," Vivienne agreed. "He might need retraining for a different job or something."

"Well, first, if either of you hear of a job you think Ian could do, pass on the info? He's going stir crazy at home and, well, they're pretty short of money. They've sold a bunch of stuff they could, like their travel trailer and their second vehicle. But I ran into Tammy at Super One, and the contents of her cart really drove home to me how much they're struggling."

Alexia frowned. "Didn't the church do a meal train?"

"That ended months ago."

"Right. Of course. So, what do you have in mind?"

"A fundraiser."

Viv shook her head, both hands up. "Count me out. I don't know anything about stuff like that, and I'm already super busy. I don't have—"

"Stop."

Vivienne stopped. "What?"

"We can host a one-day event right here. We can do a silent auction and offer pony rides and have bake tables and—"

"Did I mention I'm busy?"

"Did I mention there's a family in our church with two little kids, and they are hurting, and we can help?"

"You did, but—"

"Emma's right, Viv," Alexia interrupted. "There isn't a big enough 'but.' I can set up a silent auction. I've gotten to know a bunch of local artisans who might donate stuff for a good cause."

"I hoped you'd offer. Remember to ask other businesses, too. Communication Location might have something to donate. The Golden Grill and the Chuckwagon might offer a meal. We can talk about things Sweet River Ranch might be able to donate, from a night at the lodge to maybe a free helicopter ride — I'd have to ask Jude Kline about that. But there are lots of possibilities."

"Maranatha Inn might have things to donate, too. A night at the inn, a dinner out, or even a Christmas tree from their farm." Alexia sounded excited.

"And Monte Newman has those Clydesdales and a wagon. Maybe he'd be willing to offer hayrides by donation to the fund."

"I love it! When would you like to do it?"

"It will take a bit of time to put together, but we need to move quickly, I think. They're hurting right now."

"A couple of weeks?"

Emma blinked. "You think we could do it that soon?"

"Sure. I know you two are working—" Alexia eyed Vivienne "—but I can put the legwork in. I needed a project."

"The community sure came together to help us build that trail a few weeks ago. I think they'll really kick in for the Phillipses."

Vivienne had been silent since her initial protest. Now she heaved an enormous sigh. "Fine. Tell me what day, and

I'll ask for it off. I'm not sure how much help I'd be planning. I don't know this town the way you guys do."

That part was true. Vivienne had been here for her senior year of high school and then gone away to college. Jewel Lake wasn't her home the way it was for the twins.

Alexia pulled up the calendar app on her phone. They checked the church and town calendars then selected the second Saturday of September. Vivienne would move into her house September first, and Alexia's place should be finished by the middle of the month. The sisters had plenty to do these days, but helping others needed to remain a priority.

Emma wasn't doing this because Tammy was Josh's sister, but because Tammy and Ian were family in Christ. Because Tammy had sacrificially taken a day to help build a trail here at Happy Trails.

Might it also be a way to show Josh that she regretted yelling at him? Yeah, she had yet to actually apologize for that. She needed to. Her conscience was jabbing hard, but she didn't know what to say or how to keep her emotions in check.

Somehow, she needed to be the one to ask him if he'd consider donating his stash of wrought iron objects to help his sister's family. The fundraiser meant she had a deadline for making amends with Josh, even if she'd scared him off for good as a bad relationship risk.

Time. It was all going to take time, but the ball was rolling now, and that was good.

CHAPTER
Twenty-Five

J osh! We haven't seen you in ages." Tammy flung the door wide. "And you brought pizza? You shouldn't have."

"It's the least I could do." Josh knew Tammy and Ian were struggling. "Then can I steal the boys for a while? I think there's a swing at the park with their names on it."

"Anytime." She blinked back tears.

He edged past her and set the two boxes on the bare table. The whole kitchen looked bare. Empty.

"Unca Josh!" Blaine slammed into his legs.

"Hey, kid." Josh flexed his tickle fingers, and Blaine darted away, giggling.

"Is that cheese pizza, Unca Josh?" Soren danced in front of him. "When can we ride with Miss Emma again? I wanna be a cowboy."

Good question, and one Josh didn't have an answer to. He met his sister's gaze.

Her eyebrows tilted up as though she awaited his reply along with her son.

"Not sure. I've been pretty busy. Mr. Noah and I took the youth group camping on the weekend."

Tammy chuckled. "We need to hear all about that." She raised her voice. "Honey, come to the table! Josh brought pizza. Soren, go get Blaine."

The four-year-old scampered off, bellowing his brother's name so loudly the neighbors might come running.

Tammy shook her head. "I could have done that from here. Let me get some plates."

"I'll help." Josh heard thuds and thumps from the other room. "How's Ian doing?" he asked quietly.

"Much better, now that he has hope."

"Hope?" Josh opened the jug of orange juice he'd brought and poured tumblers for the boys. "What happened?"

"Oh, haven't you heard?"

He stared at her. "I was camping with the teens. And before that, Noah and I spent the week canvassing all the acreages in the area, drumming up farrier business for our new location."

"How did that go?"

"Pretty well." Josh flicked his fingers to brush that part of the conversation aside. "About what I didn't hear because I was busy…"

"I thought Emma would have talked to you about it."

Josh's heart lurched. "We… uh… hit a rough spot. We haven't talked for a bit. Plus, didn't I mention I've been busy?"

"Kids these days." Tammy shook her head. "Rough spots don't go away without work, you know."

Ian thumped into the kitchen on his crutches. "Tell me

about it. And sometimes that work is like abrasive sandpaper."

"Hey, man." Josh bumped shoulders with his brother-in-law. "Good to see you upright."

Ian grunted and lowered himself into a wooden chair as the boys careened into the room. Tammy corralled Blaine in a booster while Soren clambered onto his own chair.

Josh took a seat when Tammy did and ducked his head.

"God is great. God is good. And we thank Him for this food," Soren recited.

They all echoed his amen. As Tammy served out the pizza, Josh pressed again. "What caused the hope?"

"Your girlfriend is a dynamo," Ian said. "She launched a fundraiser for us to take place next weekend, and I can't believe what all she's accomplished."

Josh blinked. "A fundraiser?" Also, next weekend? Why was he the last to know?

"Yes." Tammy resumed her seat. "Ian's right. Emma is crazy creative and organized. She went from the germ of an idea to a full-fledged event in something like two days. I can't believe you didn't hear about it yet. It's all over town, all over Creekside Fellowship. Everyone is talking about it."

"I've been living under a rock." Kind of true, but why hadn't Noah said anything? Surely, he'd been aware. Maybe he thought Josh already knew. Or maybe he'd deliberately not mentioned it. Who knew?

"You sure have been keeping to yourself."

"They gonna have pony rides!" Soren informed him.

"A huge silent auction," Tammy went on. "I've seen a

partial list, and some of the bid items are wild. A weekend at the Sweet River Ranch lodge. A helicopter ride. Landscaping services. A gourmet dinner for two at Maranatha Inn. I think all the restaurants in town have donated meals for bids." Tammy wiped away a tear.

Ian covered Tammy's other hand with his own. "A couple of them have delivered meals here already. Whether of their own initiative or someone else set it up and paid, they wouldn't say."

"Really?" Josh's throat tightened. "That's amazing. Emma did that?"

"From what I've figured out, yes. She and her sisters, but it didn't take them long to get a whole team on board. It's an entire event now with a food truck, live music, horseback and wagon rides, the silent auction. Other stuff I can't even remember."

"Don't forget the balloons, Mommy."

"Right, Soren. Even a balloon artist, Emma said."

"A silent auction..." Josh took a deep breath. "I've got a few pieces I could maybe donate to that. I'd speak to Emma about it?"

"I told her about your stash."

"You did?" Josh felt like he was the last horse rounding the final bend with its blinders on and way, way behind. So far behind he might as well be running a different race.

"Yeah, she'll want you to have a table or booth or whatever. Josh?"

"Hmm?"

"Rough patch, you say? Deal with it. Don't let that girl get away."

"It's not that easy. She has a will, too." And she'd certainly expressed it in no uncertain terms.

But if she and Alexia were working together on a fundraiser — for Josh's family — that must mean she'd forgiven her twin's part. Right? And if Emma had done all this for Tammy and Ian — the evidence seemed insurmountable — she couldn't hate Josh too badly. She had a heart the size of Montana and always wanted to lift up those who needed it, whether those in need were three abandoned kittens or a family who'd fallen on difficulties.

She'd do this for anyone at all, but the fact that Josh's sister's family would benefit had to be a sign that she'd forgiven Josh.

Didn't it?

Maybe it was time to find out.

But first, he had two little boys to take to the park to run off some steam.

"That's the last of them." Emma hung the rake on its peg on the stable wall. "Thanks for your help, Viv."

Her sister shook her head. "You shouldn't be thanking me."

"Even if I'm grateful?"

"It seems to indicate I was doing a favor for you, but I'm a one-third owner, too."

Nice Vivienne remembered that. "Maybe I should be

the one thanking you that I don't have to come out here every evening and do all the stable chores by myself."

"Lex has been doing her share, too."

"True." It had been a long time coming, but Alexia seemed to have found her groove with planning the fundraiser.

"Just say, 'thank you.' I can be thankful to Alexia separately."

Emma chuckled. "You're right. Thank you. I don't know why I feel so responsible. Isn't that odd for the youngest kid?"

Vivienne leaned against the gate to Nightingale's box stall and held out a carrot. The mare ambled over to have a sniff. "Who's counting that eight minutes?"

"Everyone."

"In your dreams, Em. You don't know how good you have it." Vivienne held up a hand to forestall Emma's protest. "Yes, yes, I know your parents went through tough times. Your life was not all sunshine with unicorns prancing through the rose garden, but you had it pretty good."

Compared to her half-sister, Emma definitely had. Vivienne had grown up not knowing her father's identity. She'd lived with her unstable mother's string of boyfriends. Her sister Ainsley had been her only stability. Then Ainsley had been hit by a literal bus, lost her memory, and delivered a baby whose father she couldn't recall. After their mother died, Ainsley and Vivienne and baby Bella had undertaken a road trip to try to revive Ainsley's memories... and discovered Vivienne's father quite by accident.

Emma had always known whose child she was. Not just

Declan and Kathryn's — to say nothing of knowing her six big brothers all her life — but God's. Mom had made sure all the kids' roots were deep into God's word, even before Dad was on board. Even though it hadn't seemed to stick in all Emma's brothers until they were older.

"You've got nothing to prove, Em. Me, on the other hand? Everyone looks at me like the intruder that I am."

"You are not!" Emma stared at her sister. "It wasn't your fault your mom kept the truth from you or that Dad sent money for your upbringing but didn't tell anyone. You're not an intruder. You're part of our mixed-up family."

"My head knows all that. My heart? Not so much. Your mom has been so amazing, welcoming me. Dad, too, in recent years. But it's hard to overcome the conditioning of my childhood."

"That's why you wanted to work with kids at the clinic," Emma said softly.

Vivienne shrugged. "I'm sure it played into it."

The rumble of a truck came into the stable yard. Josh's truck. Emma's heart skipped a beat. She hadn't seen him since that night over a week ago. She might have been avoiding him, but he'd made it easy by not hanging around the smithy.

But he was there now.

Maybe she needed to take the reins and admit her faults? Oh, that temper. She hadn't listened to a word he'd said. Or Alexia.

Vivienne gave her a knowing look. "I'll just slip out the back way and walk home through the woods."

Emma leaned over and gave her sister an impulsive hug. "I'm so glad you're living here now."

"Me, too. And Lex's place is nearly ready. Then we'll get settled in."

"First the fundraiser."

Vivienne nudged Emma. "First the boyfriend." She exited the stable into the corral, sidled through the gate, and headed down the path.

Emma closed her eyes for a brief moment as the engine cut out. The truck door slammed.

Lord, help me be brave! Help me to apologize and help him to hear my heart.

The main stable door opened silently to reveal a rectangular view of the trees across the parking area. Evening sunlight angled into them, but maybe a hint of fall colors hid in those leaves.

A shadow blocked part of the view. "Emma?"

"Hey, Josh." She gulped. "I'm in here."

"Can I... can we talk?"

The moment had come. "Yeah. Okay."

His cowboy boots clinked on the concrete alleyway as he approached. Then he stood in front of her with his tan cowboy hat in his hands.

She drank in the sight of him in those Wranglers and matching denim shirt, the top couple of snaps undone. His dark hair looked in need of a cut or at least a combing.

Then he ran his hand through it, and she realized why it looked so mussed. He was nervous.

That made two of them. "Josh, I'm sorry."

But he spoke simultaneously. "Emma, I..."

They stared at each other. His gaze softened. How she loved those dark, penetrating eyes. How she loved *him*.

"I was—"

"I shouldn't—"

Josh gestured toward her. "Ladies first."

Emma so did not feel like a lady. "I'm sorry, Josh. I was way out of line that night. I lost my temper, and I'm sorry."

"I'm sorry, too. I wish I could truthfully say that Alexia and I never discussed how we weren't suited for each other but that you and I might be. I'd already noticed you. Already regretted acting like an immature teenager fixated on something I shouldn't even have wanted. Watching the youth on the camping trip last weekend bungle their attractions to each other drove it home."

"I teach middle school. I get it."

Josh clapped his hat to his head and reached for both her hands. His grip was gentle but sure. "Emma, I forgive you. You were blindsided. You lashed out."

"There's no excuse for a 24-year-old to have a temper tantrum."

"You didn't."

Was that a grin poking at the corners of his mouth? "I own it, Josh. My reaction was not pretty or godly. I'm sorry."

"I'm sensing a pattern here. I already forgave you."

"Admit I did wrong."

"You did wrong. I also did. Admit it."

She laughed, but it came out on an awkward gasp through a throat with constricted airways. "Okay, I admit it. You did wrong. And I forgive you."

His hands clenched hers. "Where do we go from here?"

"Forward? If you want to."

"Very much. Because I love you, Emma."

She bit on her trembling bottom lip. Was this the moment she'd been waiting for? "I love you, too, Josh."

"May I kiss you?" A hint of a twinkle glimmered in his eyes. "I remembered to ask."

"You don't need an invitation ever again." And she raised herself onto tiptoes, grabbed his shirt collar in both hands, and crushed her mouth against his.

CHAPTER
Twenty-Six

The fundraiser was in full swing. Emma could hardly believe the town's enthusiasm, but why should she have doubted? Jewel Lake had always stood by her residents. While nearly any excuse for a fall festival would have been welcomed by the throngs of people surging over the Happy Trails property, they'd turned out in full force for Ian and Tammy.

Beside the blacksmith shop, a row of market canopies sheltered all the silent auction items laid out on tables. By the looks of the crowd elbowing for access, they'd make good money from the auctioned items.

Emma gave Josh a wave where he stood in the doorway of the smithy. He'd been chatting with curious townsfolk for hours. He grinned and waved back but turned to the older gentleman he'd been speaking with.

She could only hope he garnered enough leads to fill the last few farrier openings remaining for him and Noah.

Over by the stable, Alexia offered tours while Vivienne fielded questions about the boarding facilities and upcoming lessons. Their sisters-in-law Riley and Dakota headed up pony rides for eager children, while Carey painted faces along with Paisley from Sweet River.

The Sullivan crew from Sweet River had offered astounding support. She'd only been a lowly employee up there, but the family had come through in a big way with silent auction contributions and hands-on support.

The community newcomers from Maranatha Inn had done the same. Sure, in both cases, it gave them a chance to get their name in front of the town and be seen with good will, but more to the point, their donations had been significant. Emma could hardly wait to see the tally raised for the Phillips family at the end of the day.

Dad chatted with Pastor Marshall in lawn chairs over in the shade. It was good to see the pastor out in public, even though he hadn't resumed his church duties yet. Over there, Mom shared a laugh with Julia Cox, Maranatha Inn's owner.

Had Emma ever thanked her properly for the donated lunches on trail-building day? Today, the newcomer had gone out of her way for the community again. Emma turned toward them.

Maggie Johannesson grasped Emma's arm. "This is so cool!" The tween girl's eyes shone bright with excitement.

"It's fun, isn't it? Have you had a pony ride yet?"

The girl wrinkled her nose. "That's for little kids."

Emma glanced over to see Dakota leading little Jamie Sullivan around on a pony. Maybe Maggie could be excused for thinking it wasn't for her. "You could ask, though."

"I want to ride a big horse."

"Come on down one day after school, and I'll see what I can do." Emma could already hear Vivienne telling her they couldn't afford to give away things they could make money on, but the townspeople were showing so much support right now that Emma couldn't help feeling generous herself.

"Really, Ms. Emma?"

"Sure. You probably come past here often on your way to your gruncle's house."

"Yeah! Gruncle Monte is talking to that other old guy."

Emma held back her grin as she saw the man in question visiting with Josh's grandfather. He definitely counted as old, especially to a kid Maggie's age. "You should get your face painted over there."

"Isn't that for little kids, too?" But Maggie sounded wistful.

"Hey, I'll come with you. What should I ask for on my face?"

"You're getting your face painted?" The girl's eyes widened.

"Sure, why not? How about a butterfly?"

"Not a horse?"

Emma leaned closer. "I don't think those artists can do a good job of horses, quite honestly. But a butterfly sounds good. What about you?"

"I'd like a butterfly, too." The little girl looked up at her with adoration. "My dad's over by those tables. Will you go on a date with him?"

Emma nudged the girl's shoulder as she laughed. "No, I don't think so."

"He's pretty nice. I think."

"I'm sure he is, but the answer is still no. Hey, Carey. This girl would like a butterfly on her face, and so would I."

A few minutes later, Maggie had bounded off to find her dad, and Emma saw that Mom and Julia were still talking. She headed their direction once again, skirting the clown who was twisting balloon animals and handing them out to the children.

"You must be so proud of your family," Julia said to Mom.

"Oh, I definitely am."

Emma's feet welded to the gravel parking lot.

"Your girls are a force to be reckoned with. I can't believe how quickly they put together this amazing event for the Phillipses. It looks like a huge success."

"Emma always has amazing ideas, but it didn't take long for Alexia and Vivienne to add their thoughts. Together, they're really something." Mom beamed. "I couldn't be a prouder parent."

"Your sons, too." Julia shook her head as though marveling. "Everywhere I turn, someone is telling me about what one of them is doing for the community. Noah stepping in to run the youth group. Blake and Ryder showing up to help at the inn on a workday. They seem to be everywhere!"

"I'm definitely proud of Declan's and my boys. God has blessed us immensely through all our struggles. I'm so thankful."

"God has a way of taking our rough spots and turning them into something beautiful and good… but it isn't easy to go through."

Mom and Julia must have confided in each other at

some point. Possibly while Emma and Maggie were getting their faces painted? Or maybe previously.

"No, you're right about that," Mom agreed. "Romans 8:28 helps me keep things in perspective. 'And we know that God causes everything to work together for the good of those who love God and are called according to his purpose for them.'"

"You're right. That verse has meant a lot to me, too."

Emma shouldn't be eavesdropping or interrupting. There'd be another chance to speak with Julia. And she definitely needed to soak up her older neighbor's godly wisdom.

But for now... was it true that people in town held the Cavanagh name in honor? Had Emma's worries been for nothing?

"Want to grab a hot dog?"

Josh grinned at Emma. "How did you know I was starving?" It had been a long, long afternoon, but so invigorating.

She chuckled. "You had that look about you. Besides, you've finally got ten seconds with no one crowding around to get a peek at the smithy and all your cool stuff. Has it been good?"

He stretched. "It's been amazing. We've got a full schedule of horses to shoe now. Besides that, people are asking where they can buy my wrought-iron stuff." He shook his head. "It's hard to believe."

"Believe it. You make art."

"Thanks. It's just something to while away my spare time."

She tipped up her eyebrows, contorting the butterfly painted on her face. "Have you seen the bids on the things you put in the auction?"

He glanced toward the long row of tables. People still crowded around them, though many had drifted off to participate in other festivities. "No?"

"Don't let it go to your head, but the reserve bids were blown past a couple of hours ago."

"They what?" He gave his head a shake.

"Everything there has huge bids, including yours. We're bringing in an amazing amount of cold, hard cash for Tammy and Ian."

"This is crazy. Who thought to set up a reverse job fair? Ian's been sitting under that umbrella with people coming to talk to him about options for ages."

She beamed. "I know, right? That was Vivienne. Hopefully, he'll get a decent job offer from someone from this. If not today, then soon."

Josh reached for Emma's hands. "I can't thank you enough for all you've done for my family."

"It's been good for Happy Trails, too."

"But you didn't do it for your business."

"No, we didn't. Any benefit is on the side."

He pulled her close into a hug. Just holding her grounded him. It might not be the best venue for a kiss, though.

"Joshua?"

His eyes sprang open to see his father standing nearby. "Dad. Hi!" Josh kept one arm around Emma as he turned to the man.

Dad's chin poked at the items on display in the smithy. "You did all that?"

"Yes, sir." Josh braced himself to be told it was garbage. But Emma said the bids were crazy high. Whom would he believe?

"Impressive."

"Really? You like it?"

"I saw the hooks you made for your grandmother's birthday. How do I get on a list for something of yours?"

"Christmas is coming." Josh offered an awkward chuckle.

"I'll bid on something in the meanwhile. The proceeds all go to Tammy and Ian? This is really something."

"Yes. It was all my girlfriend's idea. Have you met Emma Cavanagh, Dad?"

Dad eyed Emma. "I've seen you around, I guess. You're dating my son?"

Emma's arm slipped around Josh's back. "I sure am. He's a pretty great guy as well as a talented artisan."

Maybe she laid it on a little thick, but it felt good to hear words of confirmation instead of being told he was no good.

Dad studied Josh thoughtfully. "So I hear."

Emma tugged on Josh's waist. "We were just headed for hot dogs. Want to join us?"

"No, thank you. I'll look over the auction items. When does bidding close?"

"Four o'clock," Emma replied.

Dad nodded and turned away.

Josh kept close to Emma as they got in the food line. "Wonders never cease."

"Looks like he might be seeing you in a new light."

"Maybe. That would be awesome."

"It would."

"Josh?"

A woman he didn't know stood in front of them. "Hi?"

"Eryn!" Emma flung her arms around the woman. "Josh, this is Eryn Sullivan from Sweet River. She runs the gift shop up there."

"Pleased to meet you." Josh waited until the women were done hugging and Eryn shook his hand.

"Would you be interested in selling some of your creations through our gift shop next summer? Those are gorgeous."

"I… uh…" Josh stammered. The idea of his pieces being in demand would take some getting used to.

"We can be in touch about that later." Emma squeezed his hand again. "We've got a few things to discuss about Josh's business before making those decisions.'

"Excellent! Keep us in mind. See you around." Eryn turned away.

Josh eyed Emma. "I have a business?"

"If you want to." She flushed a little. "I've had some ideas, but I haven't had a chance to get into it with all the prep for this fundraiser. Anyway, it's up to you. You're the one with talent."

He shook his head. "I can't wait to hear, but you do remember I have a full-time job with your brother, right?

And having a girlfriend takes time, too." He kept the grin from his face as long as he could, which was all of two seconds. "But she's worth it."

"Whew." She jabbed his arm.

"What can I get for you two?" Sage Grant stood behind the hot dog rotisserie.

"Two hot dogs, please." Emma dropped a bill into the donation basket.

"Oh, you don't have to—"

"Sure, I do."

Sage nodded. "Okay."

"Hey, I was going to get it," Josh murmured as Sage nestled two hot dogs into their rolls.

"Next time." Emma laughed.

"You want seconds, you say?"

She giggled as she accepted her food and moved down the line to the condiments section. Beyond was a table full of snack sized bags of chips that Super One had donated then pop and juice from other donors.

Josh glanced around as he followed Emma to a picnic table. He didn't even know half the people here, but everyone seemed to be sporting a painted face, a balloon animal, food, or something else. Jewel Lake had truly come together for Tammy and Ian. Where was his sister, anyway?

He settled next to Emma. "Have you seen Tammy lately?"

"She was in line for a pony ride with the boys half an hour ago." Emma looked around. "I don't see her now, though. Oh, wait. Over by Ian."

"I can't imagine how they feel right now."

"Hopefully like Jewel Lake has their backs." Emma's face was smug as she chomped the end from her hot dog.

"It's a pretty great little town, that's for sure. I can't think why I ever might have wanted to live somewhere else."

"You did? Hopefully not anymore, or this thing between you and me?" She toggled her finger between the two of them. "This thing is over."

He wrapped his arm around her shoulder and pulled her close to his side. "This thing is *not* over, because I'm not going anywhere. Jewel Lake is home. Creekside Fellowship is home." And, maybe, one day, Happy Trails would be home, too.

CHAPTER
Twenty-Seven

"Congrats, sis. It looks good." Noah leaned his elbows on the railing around Emma's deck and looked out at the grove of trees between her house and the stable.

She grinned up at her big brother. "Thank you. I love this house. I love Happy Trails."

"And you're even okay with having a farrier onsite?"

She tapped her chin, pretending his question required thought. "The horses will appreciate immediate attention, I'm sure."

"Think you can handle it being Josh?" Laughing, Noah winced away from her shove on his shoulder.

"You think you're so funny."

"Yeah, I do." He chuckled. "Honestly, I wasn't trying to set Josh up with one of my sisters. Never even crossed my mind that it could become uncomfortable."

"Guys can be so clueless."

Noah's eyebrows quirked upward. "Even Josh?"

"Maybe especially Josh."

"I'll tell him you said that. He deserves a chance to get away before you hogtie him."

Emma rolled her eyes. "As if that's how it is." She might have had doubts — okay, no maybe about it — but he'd proved his dedication to her. Now they could settle into the dating game, fully trusting each other, and see where it led.

She definitely knew where she wanted it to lead, but the timeline wasn't in her hands.

It could be, though. Since when did women have to sit back and let the man decide when to take the next step? She could just grab those reins and ask Josh herself.

Emma wouldn't, though. At least, not yet. She wasn't dumb enough to think they were ready to pledge their lives to each other quite this soon. How long would that take? Some of her brothers had certainly moved quickly once they'd been on the same page as their girls.

She angled a look up at Noah. "How did you know when the time was right with Taryn?"

"Don't forget Taryn was all set to marry someone else hours before I met her. She found out about his deception and drove right past the church with her wedding dress in the backseat and her bags packed for a Hawaiian honeymoon."

"While driving into a blizzard in a sports car with summer tires."

"Well, yes. That, too. That part wasn't the smartest thing she ever did, but she had to get away." He chuckled. "She needed a little space to process all that."

"And you were right there to rescue the damsel in distress."

Noah grinned. "God had me in the right place at the right time. But it still wasn't easy. Relationships are work."

"So I hear." She was willing to take the leap, though. Hadn't she and Josh already had a mishap or two? They'd both been at fault. But they were past that now. They'd both learned so much about themselves, each other, and God through the tumultuous summer.

Vehicles sounded on the street side of the house. Noah stretched. "Sounds like everyone is here. You sure you're up for hosting the hordes?"

"Of course. Vivienne is only half moved in, and Alexia has only slept in her place two nights. They both still have stacks of boxes everywhere."

"I hear Vivienne has cut back at the clinic to three days a week. That's a big step for her."

"Huge," Emma agreed. "And I'll be sticking with my part-time position for now. I'll reevaluate in spring. I do love teaching as much as Viv loves stitching up kids' injuries, but the Happy Trails dream is bigger."

Noah grinned. "I hope you three do well living near each other."

"Can't be any worse than you guys and Nathaniel and Ainsley and Blake and Dafne and Travis and Dakota living in your own little hamlet along the ranch road."

"Works out good for minding the kids."

Emma touched Noah's arm. "I'm sorry you and Taryn can't have any."

"Yeah. Me, too. But it's okay."

"Is it hard, with everyone else practically spitting out babies?"

"At times. Not gonna lie. But we really are okay."

Voices exploded inside the house.

"Love you, bro." Emma gave him a quick hug as she turned toward the French doors leading back into her great room. She could hardly believe this gorgeous home was her very own. Hopefully, one day, she'd share it with Josh and maybe two or three littles, but if not? She could take a page from Noah's book and accept God's path. It would be hard, though.

Noah followed her inside.

"Hey, we wondered where you were." Blake plunked a large cooler on the island.

"If that's for the grill, bring it out back." Her brothers had joined forces and bought each of their sisters a gas grill as housewarming gifts.

"I just set it down," Blake grumbled as he hoisted it again and came toward her.

"Poor you," Emma teased. "Weak, puny, emaciated cowboy."

He made a face at her on his way by.

Ah, her family. Big, loud, and crazy. Her nephews Gavin and Toby, teens now, had run off to the stable with a couple of the younger kids in tow. The littlest kids sat on the floor, captivated by the kittens' antics. The middle ones milled throughout the great room, constantly nearly getting run over by a quick-moving adult.

"Who's manning the grill?" Emma asked the room at large. "Because it's not going to be me."

Mom gave her a hug. "That would be your father and Ryder. Is everything set up?"

"I think so." For all Emma's bravado to Noah, this whole hostess thing seemed a big step in a clan nearly three dozen strong. She had to hand it to Ryder and Carey for taking on many of the family's get-togethers over the past few years. They lived at the main Rockstead Ranch, where Ryder was transitioning to foreman as their dad stepped back, inch by inch.

Mom leaned closer. "Overwhelmed?"

"A little." Emma chuckled. "Suddenly I feel like an adult, except shouldn't I be in the middle of it, telling people where to put things?"

"You are definitely a grownup, my girl. And your sisters-in-law are like a well-oiled machine. Let them take over and do this for you."

It wasn't just Emma's brothers' wives hard at work. Her brothers were busy, too, doing more than getting in the way. Nathaniel and Travis set up long folding tables out in the yard while Adam and Blake hauled stacks of folding chairs around the side of the house.

In her mind's eye, Emma could see Josh fitting right in. He already knew Noah well, but the others would welcome him, too. Right?

"Are you expecting anyone else?"

Emma blew out a breath. "I invited Josh." Which might be some sort of trial by fire.

"Good." Mom sounded pleased.

"I hope he isn't scared off by everyone."

Mom laughed. "It's not like he doesn't know what he's getting into. But, to the uninitiated, this crew really is a lot."

"Did you ever imagine, way back after your first husband died, that something like this might be in your future?"

Tears misted in Mom's eyes as she shook her head slightly. "Never. I thought my life had ended with Joe's death, but I had three young boys to care for and a ranch that Joe's brother seemed determined to get his hands on. Marrying your father seemed my only way out, but I never expected to love him."

Emma squeezed her mother to her side. "Thank you for standing by Dad. I know it hasn't been easy."

"I left him for a while."

"But you didn't give up on him."

"That was all God. Keep Him first, sweetheart. He'll never let you down."

Emma's gaze drew to movement by the door. Josh stood there with his cowboy hat in his hands.

Mom gave her a little nudge. "Go get your man."

There had been hundreds of people through Happy Trails yesterday at the fundraiser. Josh had found that mildly disorienting, but he'd been glad to be there for his sister's sake. It had also been fun to see Emma in her element making things happen.

But this? A row of Cavanagh trucks lined Sisters Close. Taryn had painted an official sign for the cul-de-sac, and Noah had installed it at the corner.

What the heck was Josh doing here on the edge of this massive family? Emma, he loved. He knew Noah and Alexia. He knew the others at least a little. But there were just so many of them. When his family got together, it was his grandparents, his dad and stepmom, Tammy's family, and him. A grand total of nine people.

The great room of Emma's house thronged with adults and kids in barely controlled chaos. He could hear more voices from the deck beyond.

If he were going to have second thoughts, this would be the time to run. But then his gaze snagged on Emma standing with her mother near the fireplace. Her face lit up when their eyes connected.

She was so beautiful, like sunshine breaking through after weeks — months, or even years — of thick fog. And she had inner beauty that far outshone her pretty face and gentle curves.

She loved him. He loved her. And he wasn't going to be intimidated by her family. Even now, Kathryn smiled at him across the room as Emma wended her way toward him. He hung his hat on the wrought-iron rack and turned to catch Emma in his arms.

She wrapped her arms around him and nestled against his chest.

What was he worried about? Yes, her family was large and boisterous, but they didn't live with her every day. Here at Happy Trails, it was just her and her sisters. In this house? Just her. And hopefully, someday, him.

"I'm glad you could make it, Josh."

"Me, too." He meant it. He kissed the top of her head. "But before you drag me into the mix, I have news for you."

She leaned back and looked up at him.

Oh, the overwhelming beauty of her love and trust shining from her hazel eyes. "Hmm?"

"Dale Kennedy and Caleb Grant got together and made Ian an offer."

"Oh?" Her gaze sharpened. "Dale owns Communication Location, and Caleb has an IT company..."

"Digital Designs. They offered to pay for courses for Ian to get certified as a computer repair tech."

"They what? That's wild." She giggled. "In a good way."

"Ian had bought a new hard drive from Dale a few months ago and asked him how to upgrade the memory on their older computer. Dale walked him through it at the time. Yesterday, they talked more, and Dale was impressed with Ian's knowledge and aptitude."

"Oh, wow!"

"Caleb told Ian he often has calls from people who need maintenance or repairs, but he doesn't have time to handle that on top of his website and app development. So, the two of them — Caleb and Dale — are starting a side gig and hiring Ian to fill a need they both see."

"That's absolutely amazing. Those guys are brothers-in-law, aren't they?"

"Yeah, Dale's wife, Trinity, is Caleb's sister. But I don't think that had anything to do with their offer. I'm just... honestly? I'm blown away."

"How does Ian feel?"

"He's dancing around their house. Okay, not literally. If he could dance, he'd probably go back to logging. But I haven't seen a smile this big on his face since before the accident. He's been so worried about their finances and depressed that he couldn't support his family. This is a huge answer to prayer, and he and Tammy are both super excited about the possibilities it brings."

"And the money we raised yesterday…"

Josh shook his head, not that the motion would dislodge the tears that threatened to form at the thought of how the community had come together, all because his girlfriend had seen a need and done something about it. "They're caught up on their mortgage now with some set aside for the future. They've got enough on hand to look for a newer vehicle that Ian should be able to drive. They sold his old truck with its manual transmission a few weeks ago to pay a couple of mortgage payments. He knew working the clutch would probably be impossible for him, anyway. The option to replace it with something more dependable and easier for him to manage is a huge relief."

"I'm so glad." She beamed up at him.

If Josh still had his hat in hand, he'd use it to shield their faces from all those prying eyes, but his hands were busy holding the woman he loved. If anyone wanted an eyeful, they could have it. He bent to brush his lips over Emma's. "Thank you," he whispered before capturing her mouth with his. Let her parents see. Let her brothers and their wives see.

"They're kissing!" a hoarse whisper announced. Several people giggled.

He'd forgotten about that pack of Emma's nieces and nephews. He glanced down at the kids surrounding them, wide-eyed. He winked at them and kissed Emma again.

"More later," he whispered.

Emma gave him one more quick peck. "Later," she agreed. "Now, my mom wants to talk to you."

Josh was up for it.

CHAPTER
Twenty-Eight
THE FOLLOWING APRIL

Emma twisted on Desiree's back to see Josh on Laire plodding behind. "You know one thing I don't like about riding horseback?"

Josh laughed. "What's that? Because I didn't think a negative was possible."

She wrinkled her nose at him. "I can't believe you didn't think of this disadvantage yourself."

"Oh, yeah?"

"I can't easily touch you. Hold your hand. Kiss you."

"That is a distinct problem." His eyes darkened as the smirk slid off his face. "There's a solution, though. We could dismount. I have it on good authority the horses will patiently wait for us."

Emma sighed. "When we get to the top. We're nearly there."

"Promises, promises."

This man. He got her. He made her heart sing.

Hadn't she waited long enough? It was spring, after all. Dating through the fall and winter had been exhilarating.

They'd had so much fun. Thanksgiving with her family and then his. Same with Christmas. They'd spent a lot of time watching Christmas movies at her house while decorating the tree she'd picked up from the tree farm next door. Too bad wrought iron was too heavy for fir boughs, but Josh had fashioned a long aluminum chain for a garland she'd treasure forever.

They'd taken a sleigh ride with Monte Newman on New Year's Eve. On Valentine's Day, Josh had taken her for dinner at the Chuckwagon, but a proposal had been strangely absent. That had been six weeks ago. What was he waiting for?

Emma doubted he was having second thoughts. They talked about the future, but in sort of vague terms. She was ready for more. Ready for the next step.

Eager.

The horses finally ambled onto the knoll at the top of the bluff overlooking Maranatha Inn and the Christmas tree farm. Snow lingered in the shade of several boulders, but the air smelled of spring. Full of promise.

Emma swung her leg over Desiree's back and slid down, dropping the reins to the ground.

"This is where the picnic shelter will be?" Josh stood beside her.

"Travis says it's possible. I think it will make a great destination for riders, don't you?"

"Can't lay the foundation until the ground warms up, though."

"Right." Emma knew that. She needed patience on every front.

Josh chuckled. "That's a metaphor for life, I think."

As far as Emma was concerned, the romantic ground had warmed up enough to build a marriage and household on... if that's what he was hinting at. Since he said nothing more, she let it go as she stretched then stepped into his arms.

"I love you," Josh murmured as he dusted flirty kisses across her face.

She growled and grabbed his head to hold it in place so she could kiss him properly. He chuckled then took control of their kiss.

Long moments later, short of breath, they stood with foreheads touching, still holding each other tightly.

"Josh, I've been thinking—"

"Emma, what do you say—"

They spoke at the same time and then stopped. Laughed.

"You first." Josh nuzzled her throat.

"I can't think when you do that," she protested.

"Who needs to think?"

"It's generally a good idea."

"Can't argue with that." He nipped her earlobe.

"Josh!"

"Hmm? You were saying?"

Never mind. It could wait until after they'd kissed a while longer.

Finally, Josh cradled her face between his hands and searched her eyes. "Emma." His voice sounded rough with emotion. "What you do to me, woman."

A cure existed for that. But really, was he *waiting* for her to propose, or would he get around to it soon?

He held her gaze with all the magnetic force in the universe.

She sucked in a breath.

"Emma, I love you more than life itself. I love everything about you. Your smile. Your nose." He kissed it. "Your chin." His lips made their way around her mouth. "You mean everything to me, and I can't imagine life without you."

This was it!

And just like that, he dropped to one knee in front of her and held out a little velvet box. A sparkling emerald set between two small diamonds lay nestled inside. "Emma, would you do me the honor of becoming my wife? I want to marry you."

Emma caught her breath. She'd never seen anything more stunning than that gorgeous ring. And to think she'd nearly jumped the gun.

"Oh, Josh." She dropped to her knees in front of him and wrapped her arms around his neck. "I want to marry you. I nearly ruined what you planned."

He angled his head. "How's that?"

"I… I honestly was about to beg you to marry me." She chuckled ruefully. "My patience left me a while back."

Josh's eyes softened. "I'm sorry for the delay, but the ring took longer than I expected."

"Oh!" She eased back to take a closer look. "It's custom? Wow. I didn't expect that."

"My love, nothing about you and me is cookie-cutter. I talked to Eryn at Sweet River, and when I saw the stunning designs the local silversmith creates, I knew that's what I wanted for you. We worked out a deal, and I've been crafting a stair railing for the artisan's house while he made this for you."

"An… an entire stair railing?" Emotion filled her eyes as Josh slipped the ring on her finger. It fit perfectly. She might have Alexia to thank for that, but she wasn't going to ask.

Josh lifted her hand, and sunbeams glinted off the gems. "An entire railing. That's what I've been working on lately between shoeing horses. It's why I haven't created a lot for the gift shop."

"I had no idea." She'd assumed so much. "But also, we've spent a lot of time together."

"Not nearly enough." Josh pulled her to her feet, set his hands on her hips, and looked into her eyes. "When would you like the wedding? And please don't say a year from now."

"It takes time to plan."

He closed his eyes briefly then raised his brows. "How long are we talking?"

She'd be the first Cavanagh daughter to marry. Her parents would likely want to do it up big. She thought longingly of eloping like Noah and Taryn had. What a temptation! But he'd been the fifth son, and Taryn hadn't been on speaking terms with her own family. They'd been forgiven. Emma wasn't sure she and Josh would be.

"I hate to say it, but I think we'll need my parents' input into the date."

Josh grinned. "I thought that might happen, so we discussed it when I went up to Rockstead to talk to them about asking you to marry me."

"Wait, you what?"

"Hey, I don't want to be on Declan's bad side. I'm playing by the rulebook here."

Emma's cheeks burned. She really should have been more patient. Josh hadn't been plodding along, content in a dating relationship. He'd been planning for their future.

She swallowed her pride. "And what did they say about timing?"

"Sometime in fall? December, maybe?"

"I can work with that."

Josh chuckled. "I should hope so. This was all your idea."

"Not all! You're the one who had a ring in his... wait." How could she have forgotten? She tugged a small fabric bag out of her jeans pocket. "I made this for you."

"No way! What is it?" He took the bag from her, opened the drawstring, and pulled out the five-strand braided leather bracelet she'd crafted. It had been quite a learning curve, but a person could learn pretty much anything from a YouTube video or two.

"Oh, Emma. This is awesome. I love it."

She showed him the clasp she'd designed as she fastened it around his wrist. "I knew it had to be something that wouldn't get hot from the forge."

"I wouldn't wear this while smithing. It's too beautiful."

"But you could, if you wanted to."

"Emma, you're amazing. I love you so much." He bent to kiss her again, and this time, there wasn't much of anything left to say. At least, not right now.

"Here they come." Vivienne Cavanagh let the curtain fall back into place. "Everyone ready?"

A chorus of assent rippled around the room. The whole clan had hiked in from the road so as not to tip the couple off by the presence of all those trucks. Even Josh's brother-in-law, Ian, had made it in with only a cane for support, though Tammy would have willingly dropped him off at the doorstep before finding a place to park the van.

"Can't believe Em will be the first to get married."

Vivienne stiffened at the sound of Branson DeWitt's voice. Why had Ryder invited his friend? This was supposed to be a surprise engagement party for the family, not for random friends. Could she just ignore Branson? Pretend she hadn't heard him? Probably not, when his low voice indicated he stood right behind her.

She turned with her chin up and a tight smile in place. "Good for her. Excuse me, please."

Branson held up both hands. "I'm not in your way."

His very presence within the same building made him in her way. She always knew exactly where he was when he was nearby. Her sanity depended on it.

Vivienne stepped around him, but then his hand caught on her forearm. She stared at it until he removed it. "Not in my way, huh?"

"Can we talk? Maybe not now, but later?"

"No."

"I need to explain about Liam."

"I don't want or need an explanation." Vivienne already knew everything she needed to. Far too much.

The door opened, and Emma's laughter preceded her into the foyer.

"Surprise!"

Emma's hand covered her mouth as her eyes widened, and she pivoted straight into Josh's arms. He seemed just fine with having her there. Then she turned and peeked out. "You guys! How did you know?" She looked up at Josh.

He chuckled. "I had my plans in place. You doubted me?"

"I can't believe you did all this." She buried her face against his chest.

Josh held her close and kissed her hair.

Vivienne looked away. She was happy for her sister. She was. But it wasn't ever going to be that way for her. Not that she'd been attracted to Joshua McDiarmid, of course. He'd never been on her radar.

She didn't want to think about who had been. Because that ship had sailed a long, long time ago, never to find port again.

Nope, her future did not include three-timing Branson DeWitt.

Not going there, no matter how he seemed to be more a part of her family than she was. He'd known them long before she met any of them when she'd been 17.

Vivienne hurried to her sister. "May I see your ring?"

Emma extended her left hand as all the women crowded around for a glimpse, oohing and ah-ing.

Josh had shown it to her and Alexia yesterday, but it

was more stunning on Emma's finger than in its velvet box. Now it caught the light from the window and seemed to come as alive as Emma's smile. "It's beautiful." Viv hugged Emma.

"You like that style, huh?"

Branson again.

Vivienne pivoted away. "It's pretty. Let's have cake, everyone! Emma, you and Josh first."

"Let me help. I can serve the ice cream."

She gritted her teeth. "Why are you even here?"

"Why not? Emma's like a little sister to me, too."

"But she's not." Vivienne rounded the island and picked up the cake knife. She'd like to rap Branson's knuckles with it. Not cut him. Of course not, that. Just enough to make him back away from her. Feel a little pain.

But no, he opened the bucket of vanilla ice cream and picked up the scoop before looking at her with eyebrows raised, daring her to make a scene.

She never would. He knew that.

If she hadn't planned an entire business with her sisters, allowed Dad to build her a beautiful, custom house, and found a job that she loved at the clinic downtown, she'd be out of Jewel Lake again in no time flat. It wasn't fair that Branson had returned to town after she'd settled in.

Nothing about Branson DeWitt was straightforward. Just because he was an attorney didn't mean he knew the meaning of playing fair.

Liam was evidence of that.

Nope. Vivienne would have to keep her spurs firmly in place to keep Branson from getting close. Someday he'd get tired of pretending everything was right in his world and that he stood any chance of redeeming himself in her eyes.

Didn't look like today was that day.

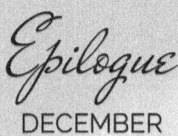

Epilogue
DECEMBER

J osh stood at the front of Creekside Fellowship, wearing a tux. Over the past months, it seemed like this day would never come. Ian and Noah stood beside him and Pastor Eli, waiting for Emma's sisters and then, finally, Josh's bride.

Vivienne was pretty enough in her emerald green gown, carrying white roses with a few tiny red rosebuds. Alexia, too.

But Josh didn't much care about them. All he wanted was a glimpse of Emma. She finally appeared at the back of the church on Declan's arm.

Josh's mouth dried at the sight of his radiant bride adorned in white. Her bouquet of red roses with plenty of greenery and bits of baby's breath barely trembled as she made her way to the front, her gaze riveted to Josh's.

Today was the beginning of the rest of their lives. They'd spend a few days at Old Faithful Lodge in Yellowstone before returning to Jewel Lake for Christmas.

Another week, this one in Barbados, before Emma needed to return to teaching.

It would be enough, because then they'd be home in the charming nature-themed bungalow right there on Sisters Close with three young cats to keep them entertained. One day, there'd be babies of their own, not that it happened for everyone. Noah had talked to Josh about dealing with that should he ever need to know.

But he wasn't thinking about all that. Not now. Not when Declan Cavanagh looked him in the eye and said clearly enough for the entire gathering to hear, "You take good care of my baby girl, young man, or you'll answer to me."

A ripple of laughter flowed across the building.

Josh nodded, gulped, and gripped Declan's extended hand. "I will, sir. You have my word." To his surprise, the man yanked him into a swift hug before taking his seat beside Emma's mom in the front row.

"We are gathered here together to witness the union of this man and this woman."

Bring it.

Josh was ready for it all.

A Note...

Dear Vivienne,

I've seen your hurt, your disillusionment, your detachment since you found your place in the Cavanagh family way back in your sister's story, *Let Me Off Easy, Cowboy.* I've had plans for you all this time. Your turn is coming, but I didn't realize you had a history with Branson until I was writing Emma's story. Don't roll your eyes at me, girl! I can't know what I don't know.

I've discovered Branson is a real person with his own regrets, but you'll need to drop those spurs of yours to let him get close enough to see that. Trust me?

Your loving author, Valerie

Dear Reader,

I hope you loved meeting the Cavanagh sisters again, this time as grownups! Their adventures with their new business, Happy Trails Stables, has only just begun.

Next we'll spend some time with Vivienne and Branson in *Drop the Spurs, Cowgirl.* What's going on with them, hmm?

Vivienne Cavanagh's half-sisters invite her to join them in building Happy Trails Stables, which sounds like the kind of stability Viv has craved all her life. She's become a pediatric nurse practitioner so she'll never need to depend on a man for anything the way her needy mother did. God, her sisters, her horse, and a real home in Jewel Lake? That's all she needs.

Branson DeWitt knew a guy shouldn't date his best friend's sister, so he didn't. But when his past jumps in front of him, destroying his engagement to Viv's best friend, he reacts poorly. Being a lawyer means he knows right and wrong, but it's not always easy to act on it, and Viv knows too many details. If she didn't hate him so much, he'd try to explain... and enlist her help.

Viv's too smart to get caught in Branson's web, but what if he's for real? Because if there's anything she can't ignore, it's a small, innocent child in need of comfort.

Blessings, Valerie
Psst: Reviews are awesome, too! ;)

Acknowledgments

Thank you, dear reader, for loving all of the Montana Ranches Christian Romance series: Saddle Springs, Cavanagh Cowboys, Sweet River Ranch, and now the Cavanagh Cowgirls! I can hardly believe we are 19 stories into this overarching series... with more to come!

Thanks to my author buddies Elizabeth Maddrey, Lynnette Bonner, and Jan Thompson for encouragement, writing sprints, and accountability. Friends make such a difference.

My amazing editor, Nicole, has been with me from the beginning. I am incredibly thankful for her!

I'm also grateful for the Christian Indie Authors Facebook group. These folks make a difference in my life every single day. I'm thrilled to walk beside them as we tell stories for Jesus!

Thank you to my Facebook friends, followers, street team, and reader group members for prayers, encouragement, and great fellowship. If you'd like to join other readers who love my stories, please find us at Valerie Comer: Readers Group.

Thanks to my husband, Jim, whose love for me never fails and who encourages me in every endeavor. Thanks to my kids, their spouses, and my wonderful grandkids for cheering me on. To them, having an author for a mom/grandma is "normal." Imagine that!

All my love and gratitude goes to Jesus, the One who is my vision, the High King of Heaven, the lord of my heart. Thank You. A thousand times, thank You.

Dear Reader...

Thanks for reading *Take the Reins, Cowgirl*! I'm so honored that you chose to spend the last few hours with Emma, Josh, and me. You are appreciated.

I'm an independent author who relies on my readers to help spread the word about stories you enjoy. Would you take a few minutes to let your friends know? Facebook, Instagram, Goodreads... wherever you hang out online.

Also, each honest review at online retailers means a lot to me and helps other readers know if this is a book they might enjoy. I'd sure appreciate your help getting word out!

I welcome contact from readers. At my website, you can contact me via email, read my blog, and find me on social media. You can also sign up for my newsletter to be notified of new releases, contests, special deals, and more! You'll receive *The Cowboy's Forever Crush*, the novella that introduces all of my Montana Ranches Christian Romance series, absolutely free as my thank you gift!

~ Valerie Comer

www.valeriecomer.com

https://valeriecomer.com/subscribe-crush

Books by Valerie Comer

You'll find the complete list of titles by Valerie Comer on her website: fifty books (and counting) in ten series! Come on over to find farm-fresh romance, cowboy romance, and small-town romance, all with distinctly Christian themes.

https://valeriecomer.com/books

About Valerie Comer

Valerie Comer is constantly amazed that living, talking, dreaming characters appear in her mind and flow from her fingertips and, from there, to her delighted readers. She only hopes her creations enjoy their happily-ever-afters as much as she does hers, sharing rural life in western Canada with her husband, adult children, and adorable grandkids.

Valerie is a two-time *USA Today* bestselling author and a two-time Word Award winner. She is known for writing engaging characters, strong communities, and deep faith into her green clean romances.

To find out more, visit her website at www.valeriecomer.com, where you can read her blog, explore her many links, and sign up for her email newsletter, where you will find news, giveaways, deals, book recommendations and more.